LIMERICK CITY LIBRAF

)

ty.ie/library
limerickcity.ie

s issued subject to the Rules
nust be returned not later then
stamped below.

20 FRAGMENTS

A F
.... Acc. N

f Return	Date (

Also by Xiaolu Guo

Village of Stone
A Concise Chinese–English Dictionary for Lovers

20 FRAGMENTS of a Ravenous Youth

Xiaolu Guo

Chatto & Windus
LONDON

Translated from the Chinese by Rebecca Morris, with revisions by Pamela Casey

Published by Chatto & Windus 2008
2 4 6 8 10 9 7 5 3 1

First published in Great Britain in 2008 by
Chatto & Windus
Random House, 20 Vauxhall Bridge Road,
London sw1v 2sa

www.randomhouse.co.uk

Addresses for companies within The Random House Group Limited can be found at: www.randomhouse.co.uk/offices.htm

The Random House Group Limited Reg. No. 954009

A CIP catalogue record for this book is available
from the British Library

ISBN Hardback 9780701181550
ISBN Trade paperback 9780701181567

The Random House Group Limited makes every effort to ensure that the papers used in its books are made from trees that have been legally sourced from well-managed and credibly certified forests. Our paper procurement policy can be found at: www.randomhouse.co.uk/paper.htm

Printed and bound in Great Britain by
Clays Ltd, St. Ives PLC

Fenfang's attributes, as recorded
on a piece of paper

BEIJING FILM STUDIOS — EXTRA REGISTRATION FORM

Name:	Fenfang Wang
Sex:	Female
Date of birth:	1980
Place of birth:	Ginger Hill Village Yellow Rock Council Zhejiang province
Parents' class status:	Peasant, non-communists
Education:	Middle-school graduate
Height:	168 cm
Bust circumference:	85 cm
Waist circumference:	69 cm
Hip circumference:	90 cm
Blood type:	B
Animal zodiac:	Monkey
Star sign:	Scorpio
Personality:	Flexible, can play extrovert and introvert, outgoing or shy
Relevant experience:	Cleaner at Day to Day People's Hostel; factory worker; usherette at Young Pioneers Cinema
Skills:	Level 2 English; typing; fabrication of tin cans (5 cans in 45 seconds)
Limitations:	None
Hobbies:	Watching films, especially Hollywood films; reading translated novels from the West

MY YOUTH BEGAN WHEN I WAS 21. At least, that's when I decided it began. That was when I started to think that all those shiny things in life — some of them might possibly be for me.

If you think 21 sounds a bit late for youth to start, just think about the average dumb Chinese peasant, who leaps straight from childhood to middle age with nothing in between. If I was going to miss anything out, it was middle age. Be young or die. That was my plan.

Anyway, when I was 21, my life changed just by filling out this application form. Before then, I was just an ignorant country girl who didn't know how to do anything except dig up sweet potatoes, clean toilets and pull levers in a factory. Okay, I'd been in Beijing a few years, but I was still a peasant.

My momentous transformation took place at the Beijing Film Studios. It was a boiling hot afternoon. The walls of the recruitment office were still messy with the slogans of Chairman Mao: 'Serve the People!' Green-headed flies buzzed over a lunchbox of leftover noodles.

Behind the lunchbox, a hero of the people was dozing away on his chair. He was supposed to be supervising the registration of film extras. It had obviously worn him out. He paid no attention to us. We were flies too.

There were three other girls filling out forms. They looked much cooler than me: dyed hair, tattooed arms, fake leather handbags, jeans with holes, the whole lot. They chatted and giggled like geese. But I could tell that, underneath their fully armed appearance, they were just brown-skinned peasant girls from yellow sandy provinces, like me.

I picked up a pen from the desk, a Hero fountain pen. Only old communists still use Hero pens. I've never liked them. They're lousy. As I wrote, the Hero started to leak. The ink ruined my application form. My fingers turned black, and my palm too. My mother used to say a black palm would cause your house to catch fire. So I started to worry my inky palm would bring me bad luck.

The office was totally full of application forms. CVs were piled from floor to ceiling. Dust hung in the air like the milky way. As I attached my photo to the top-right-hand corner of the sheet, the hero of the people dozing behind the lunchbox woke up. The first thing he did, he stood up and swung a fly-swatter around his lunch to exterminate the flies. The three girls stopped filling out their forms and looked frightened by this sudden violence. *Bam*, one fly. *Bam*, a second. He sat down again, two dead bodies on the desk in front of him.

I handed over my 15 yuan registration fee. Without looking at me, he took a bunch of keys from his belt and, leaning forward, opened an old squeaky drawer. He found a big stamp, adjusted some numbers, and pressed it into a red ink pad. Then he raised his arm and slammed it down on my form. *Extra No. 6787.*

So, I was the 6,787th person in Beijing wanting a job in the film and TV industry. Between me and a role stood 6,786 other people – young and beautiful, old and ugly. I felt the competition, but compared with the 1.5 billion people in China, 6,786 wasn't such a daunting number. It was only the population of my village. I felt an urge to conquer this new village.

Still without looking at me, the fly-swatting hero of the people started to study my photo on the stained form.

'Not bad, young girl. Compared to other parts of your face, your forehead has something: it's nearly as broad as Tiananmen Square. And your jaw's not bad, either. It will bring you good fortune, believe me. Square jaws do. As for your earlobes – fat as Buddha's. The fatter the luckier, did you know that? Mmm… you're not that ugly. You can't imagine how many ugly people come to this place every day. I don't get it. Don't they look at themselves in the mirror first?'

I listened patiently and then thanked him. Leaving Extras No. 6788, 6789, 6790 behind, I walked back out into the street. The noon sun hit the top of my head so heavily it immediately fried my hair. The summer heat and dust of the city rose up from the concrete pavement. I was caught in the middle of this heat fight. I almost fainted in the noisy street. Maybe I really fainted, I can't remember, it doesn't matter anyway. The important thing was: I had been given a number. From this day on I would never again live like a forgotten sweet potato under the dark soil. Never.

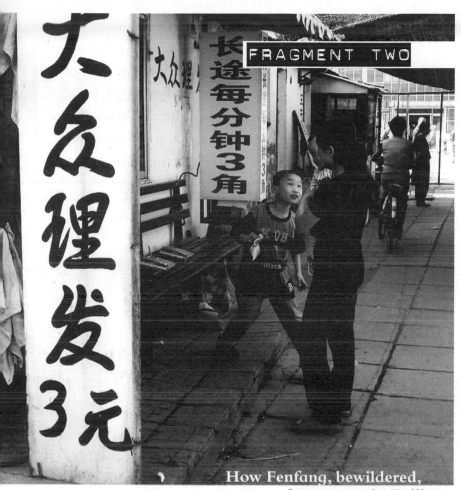

How Fenfang, bewildered,
put down roots in Beijing

My first night in Beijing. A 17-year-old who thought that drinking a can of ice-cold Coke was the greatest thing ever. I lugged my suitcase from one hotel to the next. Hotels weren't for peasants, I knew that. So what was I doing? Even if I'd had pockets full of yuan, they wouldn't have let me in. Each time I passed a hotel, the doorman's face confirmed that fact. It was obvious what those bastards were thinking: what are you doing here, peasant? I needed to find a cheap place instead, but all the cut-price hostels were in basements and I wasn't so crazy about spending my first night underground. Beijing was a brave new world for me, bright even at night. I wanted to rub up against it.

I ended up in the east of the city, near Bei He Yan, a Hutong area. The Hutongs. Long, thin alleys bordered by low, grey houses surrounding noisy, crammed courtyards. Countless alleys packed with countless homes where countless families lived. These old-time Beijing residents thought they were the 'Citizens of the Emperor'. They didn't seem so noble to me.

I sat by the road on my suitcase. Two old men were squatting near me, drinking tea and playing chess. They looked as though they'd been there for hours, or weeks, or maybe even centuries. After a while I realised I felt really hungry. Not my usual kind of hunger, the low grumble that begins in my belly the moment I get up and doesn't stop, however much I eat. This was serious hunger – the kind when you've been on a train for three days without anything proper to eat. I got up and bought a baked potato from a roadside vendor. Then I sat down again. In the sunset, the street lamps started to glow. One by one small lights illuminated the windows. There were no people about. Even the chess players had gone. I started to worry. I worried about my future, or more precisely, about my tomorrow. I got anxious.

Through the open curtains of a nearby window, a girl and her mother were arguing. Shadows flickered in the room as their voices grew louder and louder, shouting vehement but indistinguishable words. I couldn't believe a mother and her daughter could have so much to say to each other. They must be very close. In my family, no one talked. My father never talked to my mother, my parents never talked to my grandmother, and none of them ever talked to me. In my village, people lived like insects, like worms, like slugs hanging on the back door of the house. There wasn't much to talk about. I felt drawn to this house and its loud voices. I could sense something was going to happen between this house and me.

Suddenly the door was flung open and the young girl ran out, chased by her mother. It all happened very quickly. A van was hurtling past. The fleeing girl jumped into the road, her mother close behind. My half-eaten potato rolled out of my hand on to the ground. Under the van, the two dismantled bodies were crushed, along with my dead potato. There was an unbearable scream of brakes and the driver leapt out of his van. He pulled the mother and daughter into the back and, without saying anything or looking at me, he drove off. I blinked. When I looked again I saw that there was only a bit of blood on the pavement, glistening in the street lights.

I sat in that same spot for a long time, not knowing what to do with my first night in a big city. There was no one else around. The door the mother and daughter had run out of was still open, the light still on. No one had gone in. No ghosts had come out. After half an hour, I decided to look inside.

On the wall, there was an old-fashioned clock − the kind with a woodpecker which taps out the hour with its beak − and a world-city calendar showing that famous red bridge in San Francisco. A cup of green tea sat on the table. I touched it, it was still warm. In the oven, the coal was burning weakly. By the door, the tap was dripping. There were two beds, one narrow, one wide. I chose the narrow one. A flowery skirt was lying on it, so I guessed it must be the daughter's. I lay down and stared at the rain-stained ceiling. The more I thought about the last few hours, the less I cared. I was too tired to care about anything – and cold. Heavenly Bastard in the Sky, was I cold. As cold as that damp ceiling.

A whole month passed and no one came. I was the only visitor to the empty house. I spent every night there, free of charge. A guest house all to myself. At the end of the month I found a job and left.

When I left my village, it was like I took a step with my right foot and, by the time my left foot came to join it, four years had passed. For these four years I was just like some spare chair forgotten in the dark corner of a warehouse. My first Beijing job was as a cleaner in a hotel called the Day to Day People's Hostel. I wasn't allowed to clean the rooms, only the corridors and toilets, but at least I could share a bedroom with four of the other cleaners. I stuck it out for a year or so, but eventually I quit. Then I worked in a state-run toy factory making plastic guns and aeroplanes. There were about 5,000 women workers and I couldn't stand the noise and stink of the dormitory, so I quit that job too. From then on, I kind of drifted from job to job. I spent a few months in a tin-can factory monitoring the tin-can-making machines, until finally I ended up as a cleaner at a rundown old cinema called The Young Pioneers. Despite the name, it didn't show young-pioneer-type films, only Hong Kong martial-arts movies. Monks hitting each other, that kind of stuff. After each screening, I had to sweep up all the sugar-cane peels, half-eaten chicken legs, peanut shells, melon rinds and other crap that people leave behind – sometimes even fried frogs.

But I sort of liked this job. I slept on a broken sofa in the projection room, and I got to watch movies all day. Plus, I could keep the things people left under their seats. I once found an English dictionary. It was an exciting find. There was this famous high-school student from Shanghai who had got into Harvard University after learning to recite the whole English dictionary off by heart. I couldn't remember his name, but he became our national hero. I figured I could be like him – that this forgotten dictionary might be my passport to the world too. Anyway, I started learning the words. It wasn't that difficult, but it got a bit boring after a while so I stopped. Even so, I could say a few words to the foreigners who came to the cinema. And I thought a cinema was a pretty cool place to live. I spent all my spare money on film magazines and going to other cinemas to see the latest releases.

But the best thing about my cinema-sweeping job was meeting the Assistant Film Director. I helped him find an umbrella he'd lost. He told me it had been a gift from his girlfriend when she'd moved to Shenzhen, after which he'd never seen her again. He seemed upset when he talked about her, but if a yellow umbrella had been her parting gift, then no wonder.

Why did I give this pathetic umbrella man my

number? He was as scrawny as a pencil, with a sharp mil-
itary-style haircut and the cheapest kind of red V-neck
peasant sweater you can buy in the market. But I didn't
care. He told me how he'd worked with Gong Li, Zhang
Yimou, Chen Kaige, names I was in awe of. Plus, he
didn't look like a liar or a thief. I gave him my ID number, my Young Pioneers Cinema number, my mobile
phone number, my home phone number and my next-
door neighbour's phone number. He told me to get a
black-and-white passport photo and go to the office at
the Beijing Film Studios.

Who would have thought an umbrella could play such
a key role in the design of my future? I returned a crappy
old umbrella to an Assistant Film Director and, one
month later, I was working as an extra, earning 20 yuan
for a day's work. Finally I was getting closer to the shiny
things.

Xiaolin, before he got violent

FRAGMENT THREE

YOU CAN CHECK ANY CHINESE DICTIONARY, there's no word for *romance*. We say 'Lo Man', copying the English pronunciation. What the fuck use was a word like *romance* to me anyway? There wasn't much of it about in China, and Beijing was the least romantic place in the whole universe. 'Eat first, talk later,' as old people say. Anyway, there was zero *romance* between me and Xiaolin.

We met when I was in this TV series set in the imperial court of the Qing dynasty. The whole set was a reproduction of what life looked like 300 years ago. The peonies in the vases were all made from paper, and the lotus lilies in the pond were plastic. I was playing one of the Princess's many servant girls, a role that required me to wear a thick fake plait. It was so heavy it pulled my head backwards. The make-up assistant had given me a disdainful look and sniffed at the length of my hair, before grabbing a handful of it and attaching the chunky braid. My scenes involved walking solemnly into the palace, pouring tea for my Princess, or combing my Princess's hair. All without speaking, of course.

Xiaolin was Assistant to the Producer. His job was to chauffeur the Producer around, bark out orders on his behalf, and basically eat, drink and sleep for him. As well as this he was expected to nanny the whole crew. The first time Xiaolin and I spoke was during a lunch break. Every day we would all queue for lunchboxes. Key cast members and important behind-the-scenes people – the TV show's upper class – were given a large lunchbox worth 8 yuan. The extras, the assistants and the runners received a smaller 5-yuan lunchbox. Water was free.

I had collected my 5-yuan lunchbox – pickled cucumber, rice with not more than 1 centimetre of meat – and was sitting alone in a corner to eat, avoiding conversation. I didn't want to talk to anyone. Instead I watched the crew members out of the corner of my eye as they discussed the actress's large bra, the Director's new mistress, or the recent news, featured in that day's *Beijing Evening*, that a serial killer was on the loose. Then I saw a young man walking towards me. It was Xiaolin. He was tall, with a body like a solid pine tree. He stopped in front of me, holding out one of the large lunchboxes.

'You like fish?' he said. 'There's one left.'

I have to say, I didn't feel anything special towards Xiaolin at first. He was too male, with his big feet and big hands. To me, that wasn't beautiful, or 'city' enough. He looked like any young man from my village with dust in their hair. Which was strange, since he was actually a Beijinger born and bred. Anyway, eat first, talk later.

I took the lunchbox and started to devour the juicy pieces of carp. There was no doubt about it, it was tastier than my 5-yuan lunch. By the time I had finished the fish, I was feeling warmer towards Xiaolin. In all the time I'd been in Beijing, no one had ever offered me a lunch like that. It was something.

Between mouthfuls, I cast furtive glances at my lunch-giver. I noticed his rice was swimming in a sea of black soy sauce. At that time I didn't know Xiaolin loved to add heaps of soy sauce to his rice. And he had to have a particular brand – Eight Dragons Soy Sauce. He could eat a whole bowl of rice with Eight Dragons and not need anything else. Anyway, as he tucked into his rice, he told me how he hated the hierarchy on the set. He hated the pretentious actors he had to deal with. Xiaolin said the best people were the extras. Then he said to me, 'You don't look like an actress. You're not snooty enough.'

Not snooty enough? I felt offended. But maybe he was right, otherwise why did I still only get lousy roles like 'Woman walking over the bridge in the background' or 'Waitress wiping some stupid table'?

Then he asked my age, and I asked his. That's the tradition in China. If we know each other's ages we can understand each other's past. We Chinese have been collective for so long, personal histories are not worth mentioning. Therefore as soon as Xiaolin and I knew how old the other was, we knew exactly what big shit had happened in our lives. The introduction of the One

Child Policy shortly before our births, for instance, and the fact that, in 1985, two pandas were sent to the USA as a national gift and we had to sing a tearful panda song at school. 1989 was the Tiananmen Square student demonstration. Anyway, Xiaolin was one year younger than me, so I assumed we were from the same generation. But when he said he had never once left Beijing, I changed my mind. It was clear he wouldn't understand why I had left home. Perhaps we were from different generations after all.

If I had been thinking straight, I would have realised that Xiaolin wasn't for me. His animal sign was the rooster, and they say the monkey and the rooster don't mix. But I was young. I didn't think about the future seriously. I was just in search of those shiny things…

Soon after Xiaolin gave me the lunchbox, the crew had a day off. He wanted to take me swimming. He said he knew a reservoir on the outskirts of Beijing that used to be a part of some Yuan Emperor's garden. I immediately agreed, although I didn't know how to swim. Forget the swimming, let's just see the kind of place Emperors used to go, I thought. I warned him that I didn't have a swimming costume and I was scared of water, but Xiaolin said he would sort it out. So we went to Xidan department store and he bought me an apple-green bathing suit. Then we caught a bus on Long Peace Street, and we passed the solemn Forbidden City and the grand Friendship Hotel, in the end we crossed the whole capital. That was the highlight of the day. Everything else was pretty disappointing.

For a start, the place was nothing like an Emperor's garden. Just some boring little hill with a murky little pond in the middle. The scorching sun was beating down on our heads and even the pond looked thirsty. It wasn't that the landscape was ugly exactly, it's just that you wouldn't take a photo of it. Xiaolin pulled off his T-shirt and jumped straight into the mossy water. I turned around and changed into my brand-new swimsuit. When I looked back, I saw Xiaolin swimming off to the other side of the pond. He didn't give a damn that I was scared of water. In that moment, I thought that I would never learn how to swim if I stayed with him. Sometimes you just know these things, even if you can't explain how. It's fate, if you believe in fate.

As soon as my foot touched it, the shapeless liquid wanted to swallow me. The rock I was standing on was slippery and sharp. I lost my balance, fell into the black water and started to scream. Xiaolin swam back and dragged me out.

So I ended up sitting on the bank, with water dripping from my body, and my legs covered in pondweed. I watched Xiaolin swimming, from left to right, from near to far. What did the Emperor do here? I wondered. Would he swim with his concubines? And how did his concubines learn how to swim? While I was thinking about all this, Xiaolin was floating in the water as effortlessly as a duck. He didn't have anything particular to say to me, as if, on a first date, swimming in circles while the girl watches from the bank was the most normal thing to do.

From that day on, Xiaolin and I were together. I lived with his family in the tiny one-bedroom flat that was their home. A collective of three generations: his parents, his father's mother, his two younger sisters and us, not forgetting two brown cats and a white dog – all sleeping and coughing in the one bedroom. A solid family life, no *romance*, and I knew there would never be any.

There were moments when I glimpsed a different Xiaolin. He would hold my hand in the cinema and, afterwards, buy me barbecued squid in the night street. Sometimes, when we were out for a walk, he stopped and kissed me on the head. And in bed, whether sound asleep or restless with frenzied dreams, Xiaolin always held me close, as though afraid of our naked bodies parting. If I slept with my back to him, he would curl his body around mine, his arm resting on my ribcage, his warm, hairy legs entangled with my legs. I, too, depended on him to sleep. I'd prop my toes on his ankles, and stroke his fingernails with my thumb. Sometimes, if I slept with my ear on his chest, I could hear his heart beat like a drum.

But most of the time Xiaolin was either angry or zombie-like. He was stuck in a rut. Get up, go to work, go to bed. Never any change. For every meal, the three animals and six humans in Xiaolin's family (seven, if you included me) huddled round the small, circular table in the small, square room. The food was the same, the whole time I lived there. Eight Dragons Soy Sauce with rice, Eight Dragons with noodles, Eight Dragons with dumplings. We lived so close to each other, every millimetre of the floor was used. The two cats would pee in a sand box, but the dog always shat beside our bed. He also kept making neighbours' bitches pregnant.

After three years, the grandmother was even more decrepit, and the two little sisters were getting on my nerves. There was no oxygen left in the room, I was worn out. It was like being back with the rotten sweet potatoes. I wanted to run and run and run.

Fenfang lives alone in a block on
the Chinese Rose Garden Estate

FRAGMENT FOUR

THERE WERE NO CHINESE ROSES on the Chinese Rose Garden Estate, but there was plenty of rubbish. I had complicated emotions towards that place. It was like having a very ugly and smelly father, but you still had to live with him, you couldn't just move out.

In my village, the people used to say that a buffalo only remembers things for a month. I think I must be a buffalo. I've got a terrible memory. When I try to remember my time in the Chinese Rose Garden, the only thing I can see clearly is Ben. Ben, who came into my life I can't remember how. Maybe it was in a bar I liked called Dirty Nelly, or at a bookshop, the one that sells foreign books. Perhaps we got chatting when I was checking out an American comic book and he was buying the *Boston Globe*. He was always reading the *Boston Globe*. He told me that was the place he came from. I checked the encyclopaedia and it said Boston is on Latitude 42° North, Longitude 71° West, −4 hours GMT. Anyway, Xiaolin hated him. Not that there was anything between me and Ben to start with. Xiaolin said

Ben pretended he was just a young student, but actually he was storing up information on the Chinese so that he could go and work for some east-coast American corporation telling them how to exploit us.

Soon after I moved into my new place, Ben came to look at it, clutching a shaking two-leaf scarlet lily against his chest. All the members of the Neighbourhood Committee gaped at him with open mouths and swollen eyes as he stood at the gate.

Ben didn't come in. He put the lily down on the ground in front of me, brushed some earth off his shirt and said, 'Fenfang, I'm worried this plant is going to die. You have to look after it for me.'

I accepted the two-leaf plant, and at the same time, I accepted Ben.

The Chinese Rose Garden Estate was just like all the other Beijing estates built to replace the Hutongs: a collection of uniform tower blocks. Although the buildings were brand new, the walls were already crumbling. They were covered with posters telling you about medication against syphilis, and scribbled ads giving telephone numbers. In the cement yards, skinny trees with pitiful leaves fought to survive. The corridors were crammed with broken bicycles. But the day I moved into that little apartment on the estate, I felt a secret joy at finally having a space of my own. I would never again have to share my space with a family or stinking animals. Never.

I had brought my five possessions with me: a plastic closet full of clothes, a green towel, a red blanket, a bottle of Head & Shoulders, and a folder with scripts from some of the crappy shows and films I'd been in. All my other things had been torn or smashed up by Xiaolin when he found out I was leaving. I locked the door behind me and took a look around. A family had lived there before, I could smell. Oil on the kitchen walls, some abandoned toys on the balcony. Well, I couldn't complain. I thought I could do it up a bit, make it nicer for myself.

The major drawback was the Neighbourhood Committee people downstairs. I couldn't stand them. In my village we used to call them old cocks and old hens. They would sit for hours in the dust, red armbands on their sleeves, serving their everlasting socialism. Heavenly Bastard in the Sky, how I hated them – and here it was just the same. Whenever it wasn't raining, the old cocks and hens would occupy the whole yard, squatting or sitting on the ground. Instead of being Zen, they would gossip about the woman from the 13th floor who had remarried so quickly after her divorce, or the man with glasses on the eighth floor who refused the free condoms from the One Child Policy Committee, or the grey cat from Room 304 that got pregnant by the black cat from Room 805 whose owner was a Catholic. Or else they would discuss how many kilos of pak choi they would store for the winter. Bloody lot, I wished their few remaining teeth would break on frozen pak choi.

Right next to our block was the capital's recycling plant. Day and night, rattling garbage trucks brought in the trash produced by Beijing's 15 million inhabitants. Next to the trash was the local school. Girls and boys in blue uniforms buzzed around on their new bicycles. At the first hint of summer, the pre-pubescent girls would tear off their bulky overcoats to reveal their under-developed chests. The boys, little emperors of their families, would show off, talking dirty and flirting in gruff, drawling Hutong accents inherited from their worker parents. The children would clamber around on the rubbish dump all day long. Their high-spirited screams and shouts were so loud they reached my room on the 12th floor. I could hardly hear myself think.

I've been blessed with cockroaches in every place I've lived in Beijing, but it was in the Chinese Rose Garden that I was truly anointed. My apartment was their Mecca. They spent the entire time multiplying. A female cockroach can produce 300 eggs in her lifetime, and it only takes a few weeks for an egg to become an adult. Cocky bastards. Every crevice gave forth a vast and mighty army of invaders, from the gas-pipe hole in the kitchen wall to each crack in the tiles. They lingered on the rims of cups, sat in my rice cooker pondering the meaning of life.

The thing about my cockroaches, they were very cinematic, like the birds in that Alfred Hitchcock film. I was under constant attack. Singled out, they were weak and destructible, but collectively they were unbeatable. Still, I wasn't going to take it lying down. Once, I was stalking an enormous one when it made a surprise move and vanished into an electric socket. There was a crackle, a few sparks, and that was the end of that. Heavenly Bastard in the Sky, these cockroaches were sadomasochists, looking for the most painful way to die. Once I swallowed one while absent-mindedly drinking my tea. Traumatised, I rang the local chemist. The voice on the line was gently reassuring: cockroaches were not poisonous, ingesting one would cause me no harm. Though, the chemist added, in terms of protein they were not as nutritious as snails.

I decided I would take Ben's scarlet lily with me whenever I moved to a new place. But that was a fantasy. It just got eaten by the cockroaches. Okay, to eat the two leaves wasn't such a big deal, but what made me sad was, they ate the stem too. The stem was about 60 centimetres long and the cockroaches only two. It took them three weeks to finish it – a pretty long meal for them, considering they only live for two years.

I never told Ben his lily had been eaten in such a dreadful way, but he never asked about it anyhow. Maybe he had completely forgotten his flower.

**A Mao drawer doesn't prevent
Fenfang from ending up
at the police station**

FRAGMENT FIVE

CHAIRMAN MAO SAID, 'We must be excellent at learning' and 'To adapt one's thinking to the new conditions, one must study'. He was never wrong. So, as soon as I started earning a decent wage as an extra, I decided to get myself an education. After all, a girl from the countryside needed some schooling if she was going to catch up with the city kids. Each evening I would march off, books in hand, to one of the various night schools, technical training centres and polytechnic institutes that catered for peasants like me.

In my Modern American Literature course, we had to recite Walt Whitman's *Leaves of Grass*. I could always recite that line: 'Have you feared the future would be nothing to you?' And I took a 'Crazy English' course, where they believed that you could master English by shouting very loudly. I enrolled in a Wubi typing course where you had to speed-type Chinese characters on an English keyboard. I even took a theory course for those learning to drive, though I didn't have a car and was totally confused by Beijing's maze of highways and flyovers. Still, I was determined to become a real Beijinger, whatever it took. Up until I met Xiaolin, all the money I was earning went towards my re-education. In exchange, I gained a load of certificates and diplomas. These credentials demonstrated that I was a useful member of society, that I was modern and civilised. Ah, finally, I was something.

When I was with Xiaolin, I had kept these proofs of my accomplishments hidden in a box under the bed. In my new apartment I dedicated a drawer to them. I called it my Chairman Mao drawer, and a very solemn drawer it was. The Wubi typing-course certificate, the Modern American Literature Knowledge Approved certificate, the certificate for speaking 'Crazy English', the driving theory certificate... they all went into the Mao drawer. It also contained my TV insurance, my electricity account, my bank statement, my telephone bills and my virus vaccination certificate. The drawer was overflowing. Mao was choking on the mounting evidence that I was becoming someone who could contribute to the modern state. In fact, this drawer became so crucial to my official identity that, if an earthquake had hit Beijing, it would have been the first thing I saved. My microwave, my Panda 12-inch TV, my Sanyo DVD player, my rice cooker, my noisy fridge, even my Rocket-5 laptop – they could remain where they were. None of them meant as much.

The most important thing about the Chairman Mao

drawer was that it drew a line between me and the immigrant workers who were only temporary residents. Educating myself had allowed me to apply for permanent citizen status in Beijing. Now I was a person with multiple skills, all of which I was expected to dedicate to building the increasingly glorious reputation of my new home.

But then a day came when I completely lost trust in my adopted city – a day when I realised that, however useful I was to it, this bastard city could still reject me. The events of that day made me want to run again.

It was going to be Ben's first proper visit to my apartment. In all the months we'd been together, he'd only ever come as far as the Rose Garden Estate gates, lily in hand. We preferred to spend time at his place. I liked waking up in his bed, pouring maple syrup on to his special pancakes that were like soft white napkins, and listening to him talk English with his flatmate Patton, who was trying to make it as a Hollywood scriptwriter. Sometimes Ben would just sit listening to his Red Hot Chili Peppers CD while reading the *Boston Globe*. It was all much gentler there. Even the washing machine was quieter. Also, Xiaolin didn't know where Ben lived, so he couldn't give us grief.

Anyway, before Ben came to my apartment, I thought I should warn him about the old cocks and hens. He could never understand why there were always so many old people sitting in the street doing nothing all day.

'When you come through the gate,' I said, 'don't look at anyone with a red armband, even if they stare at you. Don't say hello. Just pretend you're blind and deaf. You have to walk up to the 12th floor. You can't take the lift with me because the Old Hen Lift Operator collects information on every person in the building.'

Ben didn't get it, but then how could he? It's not like a young white American will ever know how to behave in a communal Chinese apartment building. I tried to explain. 'If they see you with me, they'll think I'm a prostitute. They think there are only two kinds of young women in China: good girls or prostitutes. So don't argue please, just walk upstairs.'

I got into the lift. The Old Hen Lift Operator smiled at me conspiratorially. I particularly hated her. She had this cunning way of trying to find out what time I'd come back the previous night. I never understood why the crummy lift needed a 24-hour operator, with three shifts of fat women to run it. Another highly skilled job with a certificate.

'Back early today?' The Old Hen slid a suspicious sideways glance at my plastic bag.

I couldn't bear to answer. I just wished the pathetic lift would move faster. She continued to stare at my short skirt and my two naked legs, as if a dragon lurked at my feet.

When I finally escaped, I waited for Ben at the top of the stairwell. He was out of breath and grumpy.

'Are you trying to give me a heart attack?'

I put a finger to my lips – I could sense the old ears and eyes surrounding us. Ben was probably wondering how come the brave Fenfang he knew had suddenly become so gutless.

I opened my apartment door and hustled my stupid foreigner inside. I felt safer once I'd got there. Humans need cages around their bodies – wombs, houses, coffins.

Ben surveyed my four walls. He caught sight of the pile of CDs, DVDs and video tapes on my dirty carpet and started looking through them excitedly. 'Jesus, I never knew you had such a major film collection! Let's stay here for the rest of the day. We can chill out. I can't believe it. Some of these haven't even been released in America yet. And this one – *Betty Blue* – one of my favourite movies. Hey, we have to watch that one first.'

I agreed. I hadn't seen *Betty Blue*.

'But... do you have a toilet?'

Ben looked around anxiously, as if he was in a tent in Mongolia.

I pointed to the bathroom door. He went in, leaving the door ajar behind him.

John Lennon was singing 'Lucy in the Sky with Diamonds' when there was the most amazing bang on the door. This wasn't a knock. More like someone trying to smash the door in. I stalled. I was conscious of Ben still in my bathroom, but the banging was fascist – a sound conveying force and authority – and I knew I would have to answer. I tried not to panic. Could it be the police? I hadn't done anything wrong. I was just listening to 'Lucy in the Sky with Diamonds'.

I was shaking when I opened: two square faces belonging to two police officers. They stepped in with their standard shoes below their standard uniforms. They did a 360-degree sweep of the apartment: my kitchen, my curtains, my Simmons bed with no one in it, my small balcony with a few dead plants. My bathroom door was still ajar, they didn't open it. I felt like I was about to have a stroke.

'Is this apartment yours?'

'Yes, I rent it.'

'And who permitted you to rent it?'

'Why?'

'This is a government-owned building. Don't you know it is illegal to rent it out?'

There was a pause. No, I didn't know that.

Then they went on, methodically.

'Do you live here by yourself?'

'Yes.'

'Really? Just you? Your neighbours seem to think differently.'

'Well, sometimes friends come to see me.'

'Friends, huh? What sort of friends?'

I didn't answer.

'You are not married. Therefore you should behave

like an unmarried young woman. Your neighbours have very strong opinions about your behaviour.'

I kept quiet.

'What's your job? Where are your identification papers?'

'I'm an extra – in films.'

I glanced at my Mao drawer.

'In films, huh? Let's see your ID.'

I rushed towards Mao to find my ID card. John Lennon had moved on to 'Strawberry Fields Forever'. I hurried back to the policemen – I could not let them look in the bathroom.

The officer examined my ID closely. I'd never bought a fake certificate for anything, even though you could get them easily, sold by dodgy men under bridges and on street corners. You could buy yourself a Masters Degree from Oxford if you needed one, an MBA from Harvard, even a document to prove you were disabled. I'd never done it though, all my papers were real.

Then one of the policemen said, 'You're going to make a little trip with us.'

I felt like that stroke might actually happen now. But I pulled on my coat, slipped into my shoes and headed for the door, which I closed behind us with my heart beating. Ben was still in the bathroom. Maybe he'd caught a glimpse of their uniforms and square shoes, but he wouldn't know what the hell was going on. Poor foreigner.

They led me to a van, which I realised was a military jeep. In the back seat there was a terrified woman clutching a small curly-haired dog. She looked pretty harmless, and so did the dog. The jeep took off with its sirens blaring and lights flashing. Heavenly Bastard in the Sky, it was just like in the movies. I asked the woman with her dog why she was there.

'You wouldn't believe it if I tell you the whole story. Me and my husband don't have children so we raise a few dogs at home, but we only have a certificate for one dog. We couldn't afford it for the others. So now they want to take this one away. I said to them this dog is my life, and if you're going to take him, you'll have to take me too. So the officer said fine, then you come down to the station with us. You know, a citizen like me has never known where the police station is, let alone been to it. I can't believe this is happening. Can you?'

No, I couldn't. I felt very sorry for her.

We arrived at the police station. I kept thinking about Ben, wondering if he was still in my bathroom. I prayed that he was okay.

Then I was sitting in the police station waiting for someone to question me. I wasn't alone. The criminal pet owner was there, still holding her poor little curly dog. There was also a small skinny man with bleached hair. He was from Guangdong and hadn't been able to get a temporary resident's permit since he arrived in Beijing. His criminal name was *Illegal Resident*. There was also a fat, middle-aged woman with long, wild hair like a wolf. She wouldn't sit down and kept yelling the whole time. She claimed she was innocent, that she hadn't stolen anything. As far as we were concerned, the police thinking she was a criminal – it was her fault. She screamed so much we ended up hoping they would kill her immediately.

The policemen had separated us with rickety tables and chairs. There was nothing else in the room – no calendar, no evening newspapers, nothing to distract us from our fate. All we could see was the office across the hallway. A policeman sat facing in our direction and watching the news. We couldn't see the TV, we could only hear its vague, tinny sound. Another policeman went in to pour himself some tea. An hour passed. And another. If these guys were so powerful, why couldn't they just fucking get on with it?

It was ten o'clock at night and still no interrogation. So I started my own self-examination. But the crimes I remembered didn't seem that bad. There was that one time in a term exam at middle school when I'd used a crib sheet. There was that time at the cinema when I'd found a gold ring under a seat, which, I admit, I kept. I kept the English dictionary too, but didn't feel that really counted since I perpetrated this deed in order to re-educate myself. And then there was the mobile phone I'd found. I'd definitely handed that to the boss, I was sure. And yes, I had boyfriends, but it wasn't like I was breaking up marriages. So what other mistakes had I made, I wondered, what other sins had I committed? Heavenly Bastard in the Sky, how the fuck had I ended up in a police station?

Our endless and seemingly hopeless wait dragged on. By now, the bleached-blond man from Guangdong without a Beijing permit had lost patience. It was obvious the owner of the hair salon where he worked wasn't going to turn up and bail him out. He started murmuring that he would just go back home – 'home' being 'home town' for peasant people. He meant he would give up Beijing and go back to planting rice in the fields after getting out of here. The fat woman had stopped screaming and passed out in the most uncomfortable-looking position. She was like a beached whale, her wild hair spread around her like a fishing net. The dog without legitimate ID had been put into a cage. He whined and scratched at the bars, yapping helplessly. The woman had begged and pleaded the policeman to let it out. But to no effect.

It was around midnight when a policeman called me. He wrote down all my certification numbers and asked sternly how many boyfriends I had. Didn't I know that behaving like I did before marriage was immoral? He filled me in on what my neighbours had been saying, about how I'd been bringing a foreign man to my residence. He ordered me to move out of my place immediately, the very next day. If I didn't, the state could not be held responsible for anything that might happen to me. It

44

was this last sentence that really did it for me. The true power of Justice in Beijing.

It was only as I was leaving that I finally understood what it had all been about. On the steps outside, I overheard one policeman saying to another, 'So, she didn't have anything to do with the supermarket murder then.' The other policeman leant towards him conspiratorially. 'Don't worry, she deserved it anyway. She's no good, that girl. Much too individualistic.'

From inside the building came the sound of police dogs barking. I turned my back on that place of Morality and Power and Guidance.

Because I was the first of our unfortunate gang of criminals to be released, I felt compelled to do something for my companions. I had agreed to make some calls, once outside. They gave me telephone numbers and scribbled hasty messages on torn-off pieces of a cigarette packet. The message from the woman with the dog was for her mother and said:

Call Dr Wang the veterinarian.

The Cantonese boy with blond hair and no temporary resident's permit wrote:

Mr Zhang, Please come quickly.

I didn't take a note for the fat woman with wolfish hair. By the time I left the station, the police had moved her somewhere else. I wondered how many months she would get in jail.

With my shoes and coat back on, and the fear of the Law on my shoulders, I returned home. I opened my door. The room looked the same. Nothing was any different from when I'd been escorted out, except for a note from Ben:

Fenfang, Are you OK?? Call me! I need to talk to you about the future. I've decided I've gotta go home otherwise I'll never finish my fucking PhD. I'm flying back to Massachusetts the day after tomorrow.

I didn't call, though. What would have been the point? Instead I sat down on my dirty carpet and watched *Betty Blue – 37°2 le matin*. It was a very sad film. I couldn't talk for a day afterwards.

The phone call isn't from Huizi,
it's from an Old Third-Rate Director

IT HAD JUST GONE 8 A.M. and I was suddenly awake. I'd wanted to sleep in, until 10 or even 11. I could if I wanted. It's not like I was contributing much to society. But it wasn't to be. In my half-awake state, I realised my eardrums were being attacked by something loud and persistent coming from the tower block opposite.

In case you're picturing flowers, I should mention that this isn't the Chinese Rose Garden Estate I'm talking about. After the thing with Ben, I had moved to the Commercial Success Condominium near Chao Yang Park. A whole new tower block with a whole new Neighbourhood Committee. Plus these old men opposite who got up early to practise Beijing opera, sheet music in hand. Yiyiyabloodyyayaya. It was never-ending – a shrill alarm hurrying me towards consciousness. Fuck off!

I turned my sleepy eyes towards the window. There wasn't the slightest indication the sky was blue or the sun was shining. Heavenly Bastard in the Sky, why the hell would I want to get out of bed in a Beijing winter anyway? There was a part of me that thought I should embrace the day, but a bigger part of me just wanted to crawl back into the dark night.

The phone rang. And rang. I lay in bed huddled under the covers and tried to figure out who, at this time, on this morning, could possibly be calling. Not Ben. Ben always called my mobile and, anyway, I knew he'd be watching the Boston Red Sox in the World Series. His recent emails and phone calls had been about nothing but the Boston Red Sox and their baseballing achievements. He didn't seem to realise how remote the Red Sox and the World Series were to me. It wasn't just that they were 18,000 miles away. It was that I didn't even know what a baseball looked like. Was it the size of a ping-pong ball or a volleyball? I had no idea. The Red Sox reminded me of the chasm between Ben and me, between our experiences. The Red Sox made me depressed.

The ring of the phone was unforgiving. It couldn't be my far-away Ben, and it was too early in the morning for Xiaolin to be harassing me. Xiaolin had got hold of the phone number at my flat and would sometimes relieve his lonely evenings by dialling it incessantly. It was as though he was intent only on bringing the phone on my floor to life. But I couldn't think about Xiaolin first thing in the morning. It was stupid to wake up so early just to be pissed off.

The phone went silent for about a minute, then started ringing again.

It occurred to me that maybe it was Huizi. After Ben left, his flatmate Patton and my friend Huizi became the only people I could talk to. Strangely they were both scriptwriters, although that was about all they had in common. Huizi wrote these brilliant films that could never get past the censors, so to make money he wrote TV scripts. This was how we'd met. He'd written some episodes for this show called *The Kindest Cop in Town*, and had admired the way I threw myself to the ground in my role as 'Scared girl in police chase'. Huizi had great opinions on extras and minor roles. He believed it was the supporting characters that made stories what they are, that gave them their soul and substance. I loved hearing him say that. What Huizi and I didn't agree about was old people. He adored listening to them nattering away in the street. He said he stole the best parts of their conversations and typed them straight into his scripts. I didn't tell Huizi how much I hated those old hens and old cocks. Huizi might steal their conversations, but I felt those old people stole my life. For me, it was old people who were responsible for all the shit things that had happened in China.

Huizi often talked to me about the poet Cha-Haisheng. This Beijing poet had written one of Huizi's favourite poems, called 'Facing the Ocean, the Warmth of Spring is Blossoming'. He told me that Cha-Haisheng committed suicide in 1989 by tying himself to a train track that ran along a mountain pass, beside a section of the Great Wall. Huizi referred to this particular poem so much that I can still recite the first verse off by heart:

> From tomorrow, I will be a lucky person
> Feed horses, chop wood, travel the world
> From tomorrow, I will think of my health and eat more
> vegetables
> I will have a house facing the ocean; the warmth of
> spring will blossom.

I wanted to be a lucky person too. Feeding horses, chopping wood, travelling the world, thinking only of my health and eating more vegetables. I wanted to live in a house facing the ocean and feel the warmth of spring blossom around me. Not that I'd made much effort to achieve this. In fact, I'd done very little, since arriving in Beijing, to make my life more comfortable. I'd just drifted through this painfully crowded city, without finding a place to settle. Maybe I would never get to stand and face the ocean as the warmth of spring blossomed around me. Maybe I should tie myself to a train track on a mountain pass too. Fuck it.

I lay in bed listening to the phone, the tragic story of the poet spinning round my head. Cha-Haisheng was very young when he died – only 25 years old. It was spring, just before the Tiananmen Square demonstration. Perhaps if he hadn't committed suicide, he'd have become a student leader and defied the armed soldiers. Then he'd have died like a true hero.

Anyway, Huizi told me the doctor doing the post-mortem found only half an orange in the poet's stomach. Half an orange, Heavenly Bastard in the Sky! That's the only thing the poet ate on the day of his death. Suddenly I felt guilty. I felt my life was like a worm's. No soul. I was a useless person compared with this poet. Useless like all the other useless people in Ginger Hill Village. Lost in my thoughts, I decided I would answer the phone if it rang for another minute. It might be Huizi. But then it occurred to me – Huizi barely called anyone. He didn't get too involved with the details of his friends' lives. He was private, shut tight like a fortress. His short crew-cut and refined manners gave him the air of a Buddhist monk. Huizi would say, never look back to the past. Never regret. Even if there is emptiness ahead, never look back.

I hung on to those words. I depended on them.

I buried myself even further under the covers and could have stayed there another four hours just dreaming and listening to the damn telephone ring, but I forced myself to think logically. Who could it be? 1) Definitely not Huizi. He wasn't a morning person. He didn't believe in doing much before the double-digit hours, and, anyway, I couldn't imagine that, when he did get up, he'd immediately reach for the telephone to have a chat. No, he would sit quietly and slowly savour his first cigarette of the day. 2) Patton? He was out of town. 3) A wrong number? 4) The landlady asking about her rent? 5) The utilities people collecting money for gas or water or electricity or the TV licence? Fuck, the god-damn phone just kept ringing. I threw back the covers, padded naked over to the phone, sat down on the floor and finally answered it.

'Hello? Hello?'

It wasn't my beloved Ben, or volatile Xiaolin, or even Huizi with his thought-provoking philosophies. It was some unknown Third-Rate Director.

'Fenfang, how are you? This is Old Third-Rate Director, but you can just call me Old Third.'

'Ah, hello, Old Third.'

The Chinese Film and Television Bureau has a rigid four-tier classification system for Directors: first-rate, second-rate, third-rate and fourth-rate. But the loss of face that would have to be endured by someone with Fourth-Rate Director printed on their business card meant that I had yet to meet one.

'I've seen your details in the Beijing Film Studio archives, eh, and think you're perfect for my film. Can you come and join us tomorrow, eh? All you have to do is go to the main gate of the Film Studios, eh, and wait with the other extras for a bus...'

Hang on hang on hang on. I dragged the phone closer towards me.

'What do you mean exactly? What role is this, a leading role? Or a number two, or what?'

Old Third said I could decide which of the many

female roles I wanted. His film was based on the collec
tive wedding ceremony that had been held in Beijing's
Forbidden City in the year 2000; 2,000 couples took
part. The film would tell the story of one of these 2,000
couples as they walked up the red carpet together to
welcome the dawn of a new era, a new century.
However, he needed 1,999 other couples to act in supporting roles.

'Right, I see.'

I wanted to hang up. I hadn't put any money in my
meter and it was about four degrees in my flat. I had
nothing on and my teeth were chattering. What's more, I
could guess where Old Third was going with this phone
call. I'd heard it all before, and played hundreds of
nothing roles. This would be no different. He was ram-
bling again, so I politely cut in.

'Old Third, I'm sorry to interrupt, but could I call you
back? I'm not wearing any clothes and I'm getting cold.'

'What's that? You're not wearing any clothes?'

'That's right, I've got nothing on. I'm getting cold.'

Old Third repeated what I'd said again, his voice
getting steadily squeakier, like a drunk on a plane who's
got his seat-belt on too tight and spots the air stewardess
approaching with the drinks trolley.

'You've got nothing on? You're naked?' There was a
pause. 'Actually, thinking about it, I'm looking for
someone to fill the supporting role of Female Number
Three Hundred. She needs to be quite tall, but I see from

your application form that you're one metre sixty-eight and you look thin in the photo and, since you're on the phone now not wearing anything, eh…'

You're on the phone now not wearing anything? What kind of weirdo was this? But the conversation continued and I didn't hang up, even though by now I was covered in goosepimples.

Old Third was filling me in on details of the supporting role he was looking to fill. Female Number Three Hundred was a tall, good-looking woman who was planning to marry a short dwarf of a man (1 metre 40 centimetres) in the massive collective wedding. Everyone thinks she's crazy, but she's convinced she's found her true love. The film would contain a tender portrait of their relationship. He reassured me that the dwarf treated his future wife like a princess.

'So, Fenfang, are you interested, eh?'

'Hmmm… hmmm… hmmm.'

I hmmmed three times. What were we talking about here? A short, ugly peasant Tom Cruise marrying a Chinese Nicole Kidman?

'Does this woman have any lines to say?' I asked.

'No, no, Fenfang, the set, the scenery, the costumes, eh? They'll be so rich and vibrant that we'll be able to portray the love between the two characters without any dialogue…'

'Hmmm. Okay. Thank you, Old Third. I'll be there tomorrow.'

I hung up the phone. As I lowered the handset I could still hear his anxious voice. 'Hello? Hello?' He sounded as if he wanted to carry on talking about me not wearing anything.

By this time, I was so cold my nose had started to run. I dived back under the covers and lay there, hoping I could absorb the remnants of the night's warmth. But a few minutes later it was obvious I wasn't going to reach the desired 37.2 degrees, even in bed. I got up and dressed. I didn't brush my teeth, in case precious body heat escaped out of my mouth. I went in search of some instant noodles to warm myself up.

The name on the side of the noodle packet read: *UFO instant noodles, Pure Japanese Food Company.*

UFO instant noodles. My heart jumped a little – I remembered UFO instant noodles. I remembered, but what from? Who from? It was either Xiaolin or Ben. One of them had once said to me, 'My favourite fast food in the whole wide world is UFO instant noodles.' But which one? I couldn't remember. Fuck. Xiaolin or Ben? I knew it was one of them, and that it was said in bed, in the dark depths of a winter's night, when we were both starving and all the shops were closed. But who the fuck was it?

UFO instant noodles. UFO instant noodles. Heavenly Bastard in the Sky, I'd have given away all my best DVDs if only I could have remembered.

I sat there staring at the box of noodles. How was it

that in this cold city on this cold winter's morning I could get a telephone call asking me to play a dwarf's bride? How was it that I could sit on the floor of the 315th apartment in the Commercial Success Condominium and not remember how I got here? Where were the shiny things?

A few minutes later I took the lid off the saucepan and watched the noodles slide between the rising bubbles. Like my useless memories floating around inside my head. I poured the UFO instant noodles into a bowl. By the time I was ready to eat them, Heavenly Bastard in the Sky, they had already gone cold.

Fenfang's village won't be found
on any map of China

FRAGMENT SEVEN

I HAD ALWAYS WANTED TO LEAVE my village, a nothing place that won't be found on any map of China. I had been planning my escape ever since I was very little. It was the river behind our house that started it. Its constant gurgling sound pulled at me. But I couldn't see its end or its beginning. It just flowed endlessly on. Where did it go? Why didn't it dry up in the scorching heat like everything else?

The river was the only thing that talked to me. My parents certainly didn't. Our house was a house of silence, just like the sweet potatoes quietly growing and dying under the black soil. Those vast, silent fields surrounded our village like a wall. They stretched across the hills and into the distance — sweet potatoes as far as the eye could see. Only the river made a noise, only the river was my friend — but, even then, I couldn't get close to it.

I used to imagine the source of the river. Some faraway, hidden cave that was home to a beautiful fairy. From there, the water flowed through our world to yet another world, a magical place close to heaven where lucky people lived, or animals perhaps – foxes maybe, or rabbits, owls, even unicorns. Wherever it was, it was not a place the people from my village could ever enter.

I was 17 when I finally left that shithole for good. Thank you, Heavenly Bastard in the Sky. Everything about that day is so vivid still: the stretch of the sky, the pull of the wind, the endless, tangled fields, the silent little village and how it burnt itself into my heart as I ran.

As soon as I woke that morning, I opened the creaking wooden shutters above my bed. I could see the silent patchwork of fields across the hills, and the dark sky becoming lighter, its blues and blacks fading into white. The heat was already rising, the kind of heat that kept the village still and unchanged. It weighed down so heavily that it nearly suffocated, making it hard to breathe. A person could melt in that kind of heat. Like an iceberg, I desperately feared it.

From the window, I could make out every single leaf on every single sweet potato plant. Each leaf had shuddered in the wind on any given yesterday. Each cloud drifting overhead had blown across those skies the year before. Nothing changed, and nothing could change. The world felt frozen in front of me, like a family photo trapped in a frame. This landscape had imprisoned me since I was born.

I sat by the well and combed my hair – my typical peasant girl's hair, rough and coarse like farm rope. I hated it. Every time I combed it, I pictured those indestructible weeds in the fields – weeds that, every spring, the farmers struggled to clear and that, inevitably, returned. The weeds were like life in the village. No one cared how they lived, how they died, whether they had joy or sadness. Maybe that's why they grew so tall, stubbornly trying to reach the bright sun. My hair was stubborn like they were, strong for no purpose. I sat by the well and poured water on my hair, to prevent my body from combusting in the dizzying heat.

I looked towards the yard where my mother sat with other middle-aged women... mothers, mothers-in-law, aunties, sisters. I couldn't quite make her out, but I knew where she was: she always sat in the same spot. From there, she had the best view of the sweet-potato field where my grandmother worked. The women sat and wove never-ending baskets out of dried sweet-potato stalks. Those twisted stalks in the dirt yards hooked these women together for eternity.

And my father? Absent. I think we shared the same weariness of root vegetables. He had left the village to become a salesman: plastic washbasins, cups, coat-hangers, brooms, hammers, hand-towels, screwdrivers, you name it.

My mother stared out at the sweet-potato fields with the same blank expression she had for her husband. Often I would ask her what she was looking at and she'd say, 'Sweet potatoes. In a few days, we'll need to break off the stalks and feed them to the pigs' or 'It's time to make sweet-potato flour for the Qing Ming festival dumplings'.

My mother, a sweet potato too. Stuck in the fields, waiting for the predictable rains of the Qing Ming festival.

Are you starting to see why I had to leave? Those fields had me on the verge of surrender.

If there was any spiritual life beyond sweet potatoes in the village, it was a shaky TV set, and a lone book. The television was in the village leader's house, but it belonged to everyone. Anyone could go and watch it. I first caught a glimpse of a book when my mother and I made our yearly visit to a neighbour's home during Spring Festival. It was an old, battered copy of *The Adventures of the Shadow Samurai* – a martial-arts favourite. The following Spring Festival, there it was again, on some other family's table. It had lost its cover, and the pages were covered with marks and scribbles. That book had been pored over by every literate person in the village – it was like the local encyclopaedia.

The routine of a small, desolate village can rule its inhabitants' lives more effectively than an imperial dynasty. For thousands of years, people have done the same thing. In our village, it went like this: if, around four in the morning, you heard a rooster in the yard singing five notes, then you knew with absolute certainty that you would hear the same rooster at the same time the next morning, singing at exactly the same pitch and frequency, just as roosters had done since the beginning of time, and would do for ever more.

Or one afternoon, as the sun fell into the valley, you might see an old man carrying an old axe and walking along the fields. He might cough twice and spit once. And then, just wait, because the next afternoon, when the damn sun started to fall into the damn valley, you would see that same old man carrying the same old damn axe slowly walking along the fields. Again, he would cough exactly twice and spit exactly once. Whenever I heard this cough, I wanted to kill myself. You see, my ancestors ploughed those fields every day. And then they chose a day to die. On that day, they would tell themselves: today I will die. And they died as if they had never lived. They died like an ant dies. Who gives a damn when an ant dies?

On the day I left, I paced around my room. I didn't know how to settle my heart. I leant against the door and looked out at the yard I'd stood and looked out at a thousand times. There were chickens jerking their necks back and forth, never tiring of pecking at the ground. Grey, skinny rabbits lolloped around aimlessly. Just outside the door was a pitiful, half-dead camellia plant that made me feel despair every time I looked at it.

I pulled the old suitcase from under the bed. It had been left behind by my father when he last came home. Inside, there was a ballpoint pen, an empty cigarette packet and a ball of dust from one of the distant, unimaginable places my father had visited. I put in my one dress, a comb, a hairclip, a notebook with Mao's words 'Study hard' on the cover, and a tiny bit of money. I shut the suitcase. Then I picked up the cigarette packet that had probably been emptied by my father, took the pen that my father must have once used, and wrote:

Mother,

I want to go out and take a look around. I'm going to find a job.

Your daughter,
Fenfang

I put the cigarette packet on the table and weighted it down with a blue glazed bowl. Then I picked up the suitcase and walked out, crunching over dried leaves as I went. My footsteps were impatient, and the suitcase was light in my hand. It was as though I'd done this a hundred times before. The hills, the fields, the well and the river – I looked at these things I was leaving and already they were becoming my memories.

Fenfang cuts herself on a piece of glass and thinks of Xiaolin

FRAGMENT EIGHT

I LOOKED DOWN AT MY HAND. Blood everywhere. A cut on my finger. There was so much blood, it must have been bleeding for a while before I even noticed. Most of the morning I had been dragging myself around the bedroom, listening to my CD of Sandy Lam singing 'I Love Someone Who Isn't Coming Home', and wearing away the carpet with my slippers as I paced back and forth, back and forth, trying to decide how best to spend the day. I remember thinking my finger hurt, but didn't bother looking at it. I was always in pain somewhere. Sometimes it was a headache, sometimes my teeth or my jaw, sometimes my appendix would ache for days. I had the worst period pains too. My body was always in trouble. When pain came, I would have a cup of hot coffee and wait until it passed.

I had gone into the kitchen with a sudden urge for something nutritious. I opened the refrigerator and took out a small tomato. As soon as I touched it, the tomato must have been smeared with my blood, but of course, the tomato being red, I didn't see it. I walked back to my bedroom. I remember thinking how ripe the tomato was, its juice dripping down my chin and on to my fingers. I sat down at my computer to write an email. It was when I started typing that I realised the keyboard was wet with a liquid that was uncannily close to the optimum body temperature of 37.2 degrees. Only then did I lower my head for a closer look and see that my finger was cut and bloody.

Dear Mr Wong

Thanks for your enquiry. I'm gratified that you liked my performance as Female Number Three Hundred in the film *The Collective Wedding* and I'm impressed that you managed to find my name in the list of 2,000 brides.
I would be happy to accept the role of Woman Waiting on the Platform and will come to your studio at the time requested.

Yours sincerely, Fenfang

I bashed out this pathetic message and stood up again. I knew where the cut came from. A piece of glass had lodged itself in my finger. A week ago there had been glass all over my apartment, sharp shards of it stuck deep in my carpet. I could still hear Xiaolin's screaming. He repeated his words like a madman: 'Why aren't you answering the phone are you going out with other men are you sleeping together I don't care if it's over I still love you and I am not going to let you have a new life you will not be happy I'm not happy so you won't be happy we'll be destroyed together.'

After a while, I had to say something.

'Heavenly Bastard in the Sky, Xiaolin, I wanted to put an end to all this. You have to see someone, you stupid man, a doctor or a psychologist, you have to. You can't build your life on top of my flesh. You aren't the only one who's hurting, you know. It hurts whenever people end things. You're not more unlucky than other people and I'm not more cruel than anyone else. I was just the one to break things first…'

Xiaolin got even more irritated. His eyes made a survey of my room. I could tell he needed to do something with his body. His eyes stopped at my green canvas chair. A director's chair, as film crews call them, foldable and handy on set. I thought it would suit my life too, foldable and handy whenever I needed to move.

Suddenly the director's chair was a blur of green canvas, flying through the air straight for me. Its path was blocked by the light fixture hanging from the ceiling. The room flashed and pieces of glass danced magnificently in the air. Then the broken chair was lying on the ground. It was over in seconds. All that was left was a mess of glinting fragments on my bed, my desk, my books, my carpet. Xiaolin stood back and admired his masterpiece.

'This is the price you have to pay for leaving me,' he said. Then he walked out. Oh, I wanted him to die.

I spent the next two days crawling over my carpet, shaking out my duvet and wiping the surfaces of my shabby furniture as I cleaned up leftovers from the magnificent glass party. I kept finding blood on the bottoms of my feet. For every shard of glass I pulled from my skin, another would find its way in.

It was on one of these days, as I was extracting a piece of glass from the arch of my left foot, that Ben called.

'Hey, Fenfang, how are you doing? It's eleven o'clock here in Boston. I'm getting ready for bed. What are you up to?'

I was holding the phone and staring at the piece of glass that I'd just removed from my foot. It glowed in the light from my mobile. 'Ben,' I said, 'I've been tidying my apartment. I was just cleaning the carpet when you called.'

His voice came back. 'Fenfang. I miss you.'

I turned off the phone, and sat still and quiet in my room, my feet resting on glass splinters stuck in the carpet. I had this great urge to cry, but I didn't want to cry alone. For a really good cry, I needed a man's shoulder.

FRAGMENT NINE

Fenfang sits on the edge of a swimming pool
but doesn't get in

I've never been to the Sahara Desert, but I don't think it can be that different to a Beijing summer. It was two o'clock in the afternoon and the air in my apartment was hot and stifling. Any moisture in the flat had evaporated weeks ago. I lay on my bed. My body felt dead, my eyes would hardly open. I was vaguely aware of sunlight filtering through the orange curtains and a book in my hand. I lifted my arm and saw a rumpled copy of Kafka's biography.

Through the tightly shut window, the sounds of the city were still audible. I could pick out details. A woman shouting. Street sellers hustling. A baby crying unbearably loudly. Some kids playing video games. The sounds were exhausting. I couldn't face the day. I didn't have the energy. Whenever I went out into the street, I would find others living positively and happily. They firmly believed in their lives, while I was always drifting and believed in nothing. I often thought about Huizi's favourite poem, 'Facing the Ocean, the Warmth of Spring is Blossoming'. Its second verse went like this:

From tomorrow, I will write to my family
Tell them I am settled, I am calm
A warmth will radiate through my life
It will radiate to everyone in this world.
From tomorrow, each river and each mountain
Will be given a new and tender name.

Facing the ocean, the warmth of spring will blossom, but only from tomorrow. Tomorrow, tomorrow, it would all happen tomorrow. And what about today?

The sheets were damp with sweat. I needed to get out of my stale apartment. I decided I would go to the local swimming pool. I finally left the bed, and padded around in bare feet until I found a dress in a pile of dirty clothes. It was dull and faded, not a very exciting style. I got my apple-green swimsuit and a pair of goggles, shoved them into a bag and walked out.

The street was crammed with cars. It seemed ignorant still to be calling China a third-world country when there were traffic jams everywhere in Beijing. It didn't matter if it was morning or afternoon or the middle of the night, you would always find a sea of trucks and vans and cars – green state-operated cabs, crowded minibuses, private cars with their tan leather interiors and dogs on the back seat. But not only was Beijing flooded with cars, it was a city of smoke. A city of smokers. People worried about cancer, but they still kept puffing – many actively, many more passively. You could walk from North Tai Ping

Zhuang over to the North Entrance of He Ping Street, and you may as well have smoked your way through two packs of Camels. You smoked the taxi driver's smoke as he spun sharply around a corner, you smoked the local party leader's smoke as he tried to establish order at a meeting, you smoked your boyfriend's smoke whether he loved you or not. Chinese-made cigarettes, foreign imports, dodgy rip-offs. The city was in a permanent fog.

The fresh air outside might have been practically non-existent, but at least I was heading for the swimming pool. I flagged down a passing taxi and hopped in. Catching a glimpse of myself in the driver's rear-view mirror, I noticed how dry my lips were, and how grey and spotty my skin. A woman who looked like this brought absolutely no colour to a city. However long she sat in a bar or café, she'd find it impossible to engage even the loneliest bastard in conversation.

We arrived at the pool and I felt relieved. There wasn't much competition here. Just average bums and thighs. The swimming pool was a place of escape where flabby bodies bobbed up and down, a hundred metres this way, a hundred metres back. Up and down and still nothing to show for their efforts.

In the female changing room, I started to undress. The conversations of the women around me filled the air.

'My son is just like his father,' said one, her yellow bikini tight over bulging flesh. Her skin looked like dried fish, scaly and not yet pickled. 'He never does anything for me, but what can I do? He just wants to drive the car. Drive around aimlessly, just like his father. And when he's at home it's those computer games. What can you do with a child who doesn't love his mother? He should be on my side, protecting me. What if my husband had an affair? My son would side with him, and I would be left with nothing…'

The red swimsuit next to her was just as loud. 'My bastard doesn't trust me. He follows me everywhere. I was in Gap trying on clothes and suddenly he was there. I went to a sushi bar to have miso soup and he sat right behind me. So I came here, to the pool, to this changing room. He can't follow me here. If he does, the pervert, I'll scream…'

But it was the black bikini-top with a towel around her middle who beat them all. 'If I'm sad and feel like crying, I come to the swimming pool because if I cried at home, I'd cry and cry and be depressed for three days and three nights and then I couldn't stand it and I'd swallow a load of sleeping pills. Or drive east to the sea and just keep going straight into the water. Or walk off the edge of a cliff. So, I come here instead where there's so much water already I can weep in peace…'

These emotional buckets emptied themselves on to the changing-room floor. Heartaches ran down into the mouldy drains. I changed into my apple-green swimsuit and walked towards the pool area. I could hear the water lapping at the tiled edge.

The pool was packed. I sat on the side and dangled my feet into the water, staring into the shapeless blue liquid. Voices echoed around me, people talking loudly to hear themselves over the children splashing. The water was warm. I started to feel soothed, almost content. This always happened to me when I came to the pool. I felt close to the strangers around me. I liked to think they were here for the same reasons as me. That they were escaping their suffocating apartments, fleeing domestic arguments and newly made enemies, running from rejection and unrequited love. The water was a caress, a comfort. People felt blessed by it. I would watch the swimmers carefully, convinced they were being calmed by the shifting and chasing of the water around them. The only downside? I still couldn't swim.

I looked at the men. Tubby middle-aged men who had started to let themselves go; young men who couldn't wait to grow up; little boys who were just starting to notice women's breasts bobbing in the water around them. The big blue pond at my feet reminded me of a womb – warm, tranquil, safe. Never betraying its inhabitants.

A man with the body of a Greek statue drew himself out of the water and sat on the edge near me. Beads of water dotted his smooth chest, his rippling thighs. His face was sharp and beautiful. At first he stared out at the water, and then he turned his gaze on me. Our eyes met. My hair was dry, my skin dry, my apple-green swimsuit bone-dry. I must have looked weird to him. Quickly we both turned back to look at the water.

Kafka said, anyone who can't come to terms with his life while he is alive needs one hand to wave away his despair and the other to note down what he sees among the ruins. I thought about the diary I used to keep. I wished I still had it. By now I would have had a whole library of my thoughts to look back on. But I stopped writing it when I was with Xiaolin. He treated it as his evening newspaper. He would leaf through its pages when he was bored, looking for stories. So instead, I kept my true thoughts, desires and dreams hidden deep within. I became a person who was very good at hiding her emotions. Maybe that was why people thought I was heartless. Apparently my face often had a blank expression. Huizi, my most intellectual friend, would say, 'Fenfang, yours is the face of a post-modern woman.'

Fenfang learns something about Tennessee Williams

FRAGMENT TEN

EARLY EVENING. 7.10. The sun had just sunk below a heavy concrete tower. I switched off my laptop and started circling my carpet. Stay in and sleep? Venture out? Eat something? I looked at the phone. It stayed silent, like all my best roles. I found myself standing in the kitchen. There was the remains of a bottle of Great Wall Red Wine in the fridge. I poured the wine into a glass but there wasn't enough to fill it. I suddenly wanted more, much more. On the kitchen table were two more bottles: Thousand Happiness Dry Red and Dragon White. There was hardly any wine in them either. I poured what was left into a glass, mixing them up like a vegetable soup. I took a sip. And another. It tasted terrible, like out-of-date apple juice.

Huizi once told me that, when a young person started drinking, it was a sign they were getting old. It suddenly felt very true.

As I was thinking about how intelligent Huizi was, the phone rang. I picked it up. No shit, it was Huizi.

'Fenfang, hey, where've you been? You've been missed.'

'Have I?'

'Of course. What are you doing now?'

'Me? Nothing, I'm not doing anything. But I've just started drinking wine. Maybe it'll help me sleep. You know I haven't been able to sleep for days. I only manage to drop off when everyone else goes to work in the morning. I wish I had an internal clock like other people...'

'All right, Fenfang, stop drinking,' said Huizi. 'Listen, I've just finished the first draft of a TV script – twenty episodes. I've been told I can recommend some female leads to the Director. So I thought of you. I'm with the Director right now, having dinner. Get in a taxi and come here immediately. We're at Sun Yue Dumplings on Hospital Street in Haidan. Hurry! I'll pay the fare.'

I hung up with a hundred thanks. Now I was moving quickly. I changed into something decent and sharp. A Korean TB2 skirt. A tight-fitting Double Love T-shirt. A pair of high heels I never managed to walk in for more than 10 minutes. And I pulled my hair into a ponytail. I looked like a new-generation woman. This TV Director would believe at once I was the actress he needed. Minutes later I was in a taxi on the way to Sun Yue Dumplings. Using the rear-view mirror I brushed powder on to my cheeks, added colour to my lips and darkened my eyebrows. I looked like a juicy peach ready for picking.

When the taxi stopped at the dumpling restaurant,

Huizi was sitting alone. Four huge plates of steaming dumplings filled the table in front of him. He was staring at the food like an idiot.

'Where's the Director? Didn't you say he wanted to choose actors with you?'

Huizi looked at me. 'He just left, literally a minute ago. I'm so sorry. He didn't even give me the payment he owed me for the script.'

'What?' I couldn't believe my luck. I slumped into the empty seat across from Huizi. It was still warm.

'It's a complicated story,' said Huizi. 'We just ordered all these dumplings ten minutes ago. Then the Director's phone rang and it was his Producer. The Producer told him that their investor, some rich stock-market dude, got killed last night. Policemen said it was a murder. What happened was, the Producer went to collect the first instalment of money from this guy and found him dead on the floor. Blood everywhere. So now the Director has to go to the police station for questioning.'

Huizi lowered his head. 'It's probably a good thing. Now you won't waste your time with lousy people.'

I didn't know what to say. I leant over, picked up the clean chopsticks in front of me and reached out for a fennel dumpling. Heavenly Bastard in the Sky, there was a bottle of Eight Dragons Soy Sauce on the table. I couldn't believe my eyes. What sort of Director had been sitting here? Deep down, I'd always suspected there was a link between the high salt content in Eight Dragons Soy

Sauce and Xiaolin's temper. Anyway, what the hell. I poured some of the damn soy sauce on to my plate, dipped the dumpling in it and swallowed without chewing. I was starving, and apparently I'd just lost my one opportunity to play a leading role. At least I could eat, eat as much as I could, eat until the world didn't owe me one penny.

After about 10 dumplings, I stopped feeling low. At least Huizi and I had each other to share this bizarre moment. At least I wasn't alone. I was thankful for that, Heavenly Bastard in the Sky.

Huizi sat back, watching me eat. I finished the whole plate of fennel dumplings, and started on the pork and chive ones.

'Fenfang, maybe this is a sign,' he said. 'Maybe you need to try something other than acting. You like reading. You know about films. Why don't you try to write a script? Seriously, if you could just finish a first draft, I'm sure I could help you to show it to people.'

'A first draft?' I looked at him, my mouth full of dumplings.

'Yes. Have you ever heard this: "Don't maul, don't suffer, don't groan – till the first draft is finished"?'

'Who said that?'

'Tennessee Williams.'

The dumpling stuck in my throat. 'Tennessee Williams? Who's that?'

'He's this American playwright who came from

Mississippi, where there are loads of tornadoes during the summer. You know tornadoes?' Huizi asked. 'They're like typhoons, lots of crazy wind and wild rain. Anyway, he wrote a famous play called *A Streetcar Named Desire.*'

Desire? That was a weird name for a car. I imagined that Tennessee Williams was from some shiny world swept by dramatic winds.

Tornadoes, desire... these words excited me. Even though I'd never heard of Tennessee Williams, I clung to everything Huizi told me. I polished off the pork and chive dumplings, and felt encouraged.

'Huizi,' I said, 'you've got to be my best friend in the whole world. If everyone else on the planet died, I wouldn't give a shit. Even my mother. But if you died, I'd howl.'

Fenfang befriends a humble man called Hao An

EVERYTHING AROUND ME WAS CHANGING so fast – my apartment block, the local shops, the alleys, the roads, the subway lines. Beijing was moving forwards like an express train, but my life was going nowhere. Okay, so I was getting lots of work, but it was all the same. Woman Waiting on the Platform, Lady in Waiting, Bored Waitress. I was only in my twenties, but I felt 70. I had to do something, ask my brain to start working, so I could match this fast-moving city.

Inspired by Huizi, I started to watch nameless men and women in the street. We were alike: none of us heroes, just ordinary people – extras – drifting through messy streets in a vast, messy Beijing. One morning, I went for a walk along the rubble-filled roads near my building. The area was being completely reconstructed. Three or four giant trucks had just arrived to start their demolition. Old buildings were going. Entire streets were going. In just one night all the food stalls had disappeared, along with the men from the countryside who used to run them.

A man came to my mind. An ordinary man who had once moved through these empty streets. He could have had any name. I decided that he was called Hao An.

Hao An was nothing special to look at. Just an average nobody, unmemorable. The moment I thought of him, I felt like I'd heard about him before. I was sure he'd been mentioned in the scraps of gossip I picked up as I wandered around the neighbourhood. I started to write.

When I finally finished the story, I was nervous of showing it to Huizi. What if he thought it was a piece of shit? What if the producers he knew thought he was insane for trying to help such a fucking awful writer? Then I remembered the Assistant Director – the man with the pathetic yellow umbrella and the bible of useful names. He'd worked his way up through the ranks to become a prominent Second-Rate Director. Perhaps he would read my script. I gave him a call.

We met in Serve the People, the one on Electronics Street, because the Second-Rate Director wanted to eat Thai food. He looked different: fatter, with a ponytail and meticulously trimmed beard. Despite this, the pitiful red V-neck peasant sweater still peeped out from inside his jacket. Over pork and rice, I tried hard to sell the story of Hao An to the Second-Rate Director, but he didn't even let me finish. He shook his head and said this wasn't the kind of film people wanted to see. There was no moral, no uplifting message. Couldn't there be a mention of Red Army Day? Or National Tree Planting Day? Or China Aids Day? No? And what was he called – Hao An? Why such a boring name? Far too humble and unfashionable-sounding. My hero did absolutely nothing of value in the course of the story. He didn't represent the 21st-century Chinese. How could he, a Second-Rate Director, cast such a film? There was no way stars like Little Swallow, Su Youpeng or Xu Jinglei would be in something like this. It just wasn't *modern* enough. The Second-Rate Director repeated the word 'modern' in English, just to make his point.

I went back to my flat and lay down on my bed with all my clothes on. For two hours I didn't move. What had Huizi been thinking? There was no way I could write a script if I had no idea what would pull in an audience. From the way the Second-Rate Director had talked, it seemed like I would be better off studying for an MBA before I wrote a word. Clearly I was no Bo Le, the legendary horseman with an instinctive knowledge of horses. Bo Le always chose the right horses to win battles, but Hao An's story was a donkey. I wasn't even fit to be Bo Le's assistant.

Still, I couldn't stop thinking about Hao An and his trivial life.

THE SEVEN REINCARNATIONS OF HAO AN

SETTING
Beijing. 1999—2000. The last couple of months before the millennium.

DESCRIPTION OF MAIN CHARACTER
It's difficult to tell you what Hao An looks like. He's so ordinary, he's like a grain of sand in the gutter of a road in a big city. Let's just say he looks like any man who has grown up in a small, rural village in China and then moved to the city. He has no skills and no clue. His age? Hard to tell. He could be 30, he could be over 40. His body-language is self-effacing; his past is vague.

The first job Hao An got when he arrived in the city was as a driving instructor — making use of his 10 years' experience driving a tractor through sugar-cane fields. He wore a standard-issue blue uniform and sat behind the wheel of a Liberation 1041 truck. He blended right in. Next he worked in a factory moulding metal screws. He was a model worker and could mould twice as many screws as any other worker. But when the warehouse became over-stocked with metal screws and the state was unable to sell them, Hao An wasn't seen as such a model worker after all.

But that is irrelevant to this story, which begins

as the new millennium is tapping Hao An on the
shoulder. He is unemployed. He has a place to stay,
but not really a home. He doesn't smile. The filth
and dust of hard living have become ingrained in
the lines of his face. He doesn't have any friends,
but he isn't lonely. The day-to-day grind of
earning enough to eat keeps him too busy for that.

The film starts like this.

Scene I

On a forgotten road in Beijing, a woman with a pow-
dered face and bright-red lips bites into a hot
chestnut. Her curly hair is tied back and the fur
coat she is wearing is mangled and dusty. She looks
like she spent the night somewhere unfamiliar. A
place with no combs or mirrors. Simply a venue for a
one-night stand.

Her name is Li Li. Or maybe it's Zhen Zhen or Sha
Sha or Mei Mei, or any other name known by the
Heavenly Bastard in the Sky. It doesn't matter. She
finishes off the chestnut and hands a coin to the
man at the stall. Then she starts walking. We lose
her in the crowd.

Scene 2

The crowd is gathered around two middle-aged men
selling stamps. One of the stamp-sellers is Hao An.
This is Hao An's third job, but he's not a very good

salesman. Turning the pages of his book, he focuses on two rare stamps (the only existing examples in China, of course): an Army stamp that was withdrawn from circulation because it had too many tanks on it, and a stamp from the Cultural Revolution that had to be pulped because it showed Chairman Mao with his big black mole on the wrong side of his face. Hao An's hoping to convince the crowd that each is worth 2,000 yuan, but none of the men standing around Hao An has more than 100 or 200 yuan in the pocket of his cheap western-style trousers. As the surrounding idlers question Hao An, his fellow stamp-seller suddenly yells, 'Police!!' Hao An jams the book of stamps under his arm and rushes off.

Scene 3

His pockets still empty, Hao An wanders down a name-less street, directionless. He has no woman, no plans, no bank deposit book. He notices some ads on a nearby wall, ads for VCD players — soon to be replaced by DVD machines, but currently all the rage in China: Amoi Electrics, Xianke Electronics, Wanlida and Wanyan. The seeds of his fourth job are planted.

Scene 4

Hao An's room, off the first courtyard in Cat's Eye Alley. The four walls are bare. No photos of women or children, no mirrors or combs anywhere. Only three or four 'Model Worker' certificates stuck to the ceiling to stop the rain from coming in.

Hao An has borrowed a VCD player from a neighbour and is going through a collection of pirated disks he has managed to get hold of. He watches each film carefully. He doesn't want to sell porn. Despite not having any friends and knowing that he is not a great man, Hao An has principles. Five of the films seem dubious. One in particular — a French film in which a scantily clad blonde woman lies on a bed doing nothing for over an hour except smoking, drinking, eating strange foreign food, talking on the phone, then taking off all her clothes and reading out her poetry in the nude. In the end she lies on a red sofa and touches herself, moaning like a baby cow. No one else appears. What the hell kind of film is this? Where's her man? Why's she naked if she's on her own? Will the police think it's porn? Since Hao An isn't sure of the answer, he puts it aside, along with the other four.

Scene 5

Hao An sets himself up near other VCD-hawkers on a street corner in the Haidian district. He uses a different sales tactic to the other men. Instead of taking the customers down a dark alley to show them his collection, he keeps his VCDs on him. Hao An's method is more risky, but more profitable. By late afternoon he has made over 400 yuan. The other VCD-sellers are jealous. On his way home that night Hao An is attacked by a gang of them. They beat him senseless, steal his VCDs and the 400 yuan he earned that day, leave him in an alley. As the sun sets, Hao An rests his bruised body against the wall of a building.

Scene 6

Remember the woman from earlier? The one biting into the hot chestnut? That same night, Li Li stands at a food stall and is approached by a group of men. She sits down with them, shares some fried pig ears and flirts. One of the men gives her 400 yuan and they leave together. The 400 yuan still smell of Hao An.

Scene 7

Hao An's Chi is badly depleted, his confidence knocked. But, as I said, Hao An is the kind of man who keeps himself busy. His fifth job gives him a brush with the fashion world. He orders a batch of handmade tie-dyed shirts from Guizhou province and takes them to a graduate student at the Central Authority Fine Arts School to find out what to charge. The graduate student swings his long hair back and forth and tells Hao An these shirts are not

authentic enough, not tribal enough. No way are
young Beijingers going to be interested in them:
there's no art, no attitude. 'What should I do now
then?' asks Hao An. The graduate student tells him
to head to the bars in Sanlitun and sell them to
drunken foreigners and pretentious businessmen
with art collections.

Scene 8

The boozy streets of Sanlitun. The people around
here are unlike anything Hao An has seen. White
boys and white girls, black boys and black girls sit
together in front of coffee shops looking bored.
Westerners seem to have no purpose in their lives.
But Hao An minds his own business. The customer is
God. He peddles his clothes enthusiastically to the
foreigners. One of them even gives him a green
American bill — 50 dollars. His day has come.

At some point during this successful shirt-selling
exercise, Hao An meets a man interested in buying
porn VCDs. The man looks trustworthy. Hao An thinks
for a moment, then tells him to come back tomorrow.

Scene 9

Hao An waits for the trustworthy man, five VCDs in
his bag, including the strange French film. He
waits for so long in the burning sun that he feels he
might pass out, so he walks into a dim bar. He's

momentarily blinded by the darkness. As his sight returns, he can make out a heavily made-up woman in the corner. She is drinking something strange. It's the colour of blood, with a limp stalk of celery poking out of it. The wilted leaves of the celery droop down the side of the glass.

Hao An asks the woman if she is interested in tie-dyed shirts from Guizhou. He opens his holdall in front of her. As he does so, he notices that her lips are the same colour as her drink.

Scene IO

Fifteen minutes later. Li Li has chosen a shirt but, not having enough money to pay for it, has offered Hao An a drink instead. It's been a long time since a woman has talked to him, let alone offered him a drink. Hao An accepts with gratitude. Now he sits with a can of 'tonic water' in front of him. Although he doesn't like the taste, he's content.

Li Li doesn't say anything, just stirs her drink with the celery stick, and then stirs again. She looks like someone tired of speaking.

Suddenly she says, 'Sounds good.' Hao An is confused. What sounds good? Li Li points to the speakers on a nearby shelf. Hao An nods. The music, of course. Sandy Lam is singing 'I Love Someone Who Isn't Coming Home'. Li Li listens with her head tilted to one side. Her eyes sparkle. Eventually

Sandy Lam's voice fades out and Li Li's eyes grow
dim once more. Hao An studies his can of tonic water
and can't think of anything to say.

Silence... then two policemen come into the bar.
They're walking towards Hao An. He panics and tries
to hide the VCDs under his chair. But the policemen
aren't interested in him, it's Li Li they want.

Scene II
Hao An looks around. The bar is empty. He turns to
the window and sees there's no one sitting at the
tables outside either. The clothes-sellers who have
flocked to Beijing from Zhejiang province sit in
the shade, listless and hot. Hao An looks at the
strange drink on the table in front of him and
thinks of the woman he's just met. There's a red
mark on the rim of the glass, but he can't tell if
it's from her lipstick or from the sticky blood-red
stuff she was drinking.

Scene I2
Beijing Friendship Hotel. Here is Hao An in a smart
red uniform, holding open the door to one of
Beijing's finest five-star establishments. A Doorman. Or rather, his official title: Attendant to the
Grand Lobby. His sixth job, found in the Classifieds
section of a newspaper. Hao An's expression is still
inscrutable, but occasionally his facial muscles

tighten slightly. Not exactly a smile, but that must surely be what he's aiming at.

Today, Hao An opens the door to an elegant man with fine, chiselled features. The man is courteous to Hao An and gives him a generous tip.

Scene 13

Ten o'clock in the evening, the same gentleman comes back to the hotel carrying a bag full of fruit — kiwis, tangerines, pears, mangoes. This surprises Hao An, since fruit is not the kind of thing meat-loving Chinese men usually buy. As Hao An holds the door open for him, the man stops and says in a low voice, 'Come to my room tonight after you finish your shift. Room 502.' Hao An is taken aback. Guests rarely even talk to him. 'Of course,' he murmurs politely, 'of course, of course.' The man smiles and strolls across the Grand Lobby to the lift, clutching his bag of fruit.

Scene 14

At midnight, Hao An, no longer in his uniform, stands outside Room 502. The elegant man opens the door in a silk robe. He is holding a bottle of Great Wall wine in one hand, a corkscrew in the other. 'Wonderful,' he says. 'You came. I wondered whether you would.'

The man pours Hao An a glass of wine and invites

him to sit down. Hao An perches on the edge of the
plush sofa. He feels awkward. This luxury room
costs I,000 yuan a night. He doesn't belong there,
and he finds the wine sour. He much prefers drinking Er Guo Tou, the cheap Beijing favourite.

'Friend, I like you,' says the man. Hao An listens
and nods. Why would the man have invited him to his
room if he didn't like him?

Later, Hao An lies contentedly under the covers
of a comfortable single bed, with the man in the bed
next to him. They are watching TV. Hao An has never
seen so many channels: Phoenix satellite, pay-per-
view movies, MTV, ESPN, CNN. And they all speak
foreign languages. Suddenly the man comes over to
Hao An's little bed. He lies down next to him and
reaches for Hao An's hand. Hao An is confused. Is
the man asking him to leave? The man smiles at him
the way he has smiled all night and pulls back the
sheets that cover Hao An. Hao An continues to be
confused for four seconds. After five seconds, he
finally understands what the man is doing and
pushes him away. There is a scuffle. Hao An's push
was gentle, but the man grabs at him, forcing Hao An
to fend him off. As quick as he can, Hao An climbs
out of the soft bed, scoops up his things and runs
out of the room.

In the lift, Hao An catches a reflection of
himself in the metal doors. His cheeks are red. He

can't remember blushing before. As soon as the doors open he rushes across the Grand Lobby, pushes open the heavy glass doors and flees into the night.

If he hadn't been running, he would have noticed that, as he went out of the glass doors, the woman from the bar in Sanlitun, Li Li of the Bloody Mary, was coming in, accompanied by a man in a black suit. Hao An and Li Li's bodies are no more than 317 millimetres apart when they pass each other. Rays of fate bounce off both of them and die out unnoticed.

Scene 15

There is a saying that 'when an old century is ending and a new century is about to be born, people's tastes become more extreme'. Spicy Ma La hotpot was all the rage in late twentieth-century Beijing, and the hotpot restaurants were raking it in.

Hao An can't afford to buy a restaurant, but he sees the potential. As his seventh job, he sets up a stall by the side of a busy main road, selling hotpot so full of red chillies, garlic and ginger that it blows the roof off your mouth. Come rain or shine, Hao An is there at his stall, as reliable as a lamp post. Next to Hao An is another street vendor — a man who sells roasted chestnuts. The chestnut man keeps Hao An entertained with elaborate stories of UFOs. He tells Hao An he's seen one in the town of

Changping, 30 miles away from Beijing: a real UFO, 'round as the bowls you serve your Ma La hotpot in'. He's convinced it's a sign that the end of the world is near.

Scene 16

The chestnut man has gone off to a classy hotel to eat lobster, steam in a sauna and generally pamper himself before the inevitable end arrives. Alone, Hao An watches the pedestrians rush past. He doesn't know a single one. But then he sees the Bloody Mary woman from the bar. She's wearing his tie-dyed shirt over her dress, like some kind of coat.

Hao An starts to run after her. He calls out and she turns around. At first she frowns, as though searching for his face in her memory-bank of male faces. But soon she seems to recognise him. Hao An slows down and points back to his hotpot stall. The woman smiles and follows him. They sit down and Hao An gives her a bowl of spicy tofu and pak choi. She tells him her name is Li Li.

'Such good food,' says Li Li. 'I haven't eaten for days.' Hao An is pleased. 'If you think so, you should come again.' He is strangely elated. What end of the world? What UFOs? Life is good. Spicy Ma La hotpot. Busy streets and hungry customers. Li Li in his tie-dyed shirt. He has all he needs.

Scene 17

It is morning in Hao An's little room in Cat's Eye
Alley. The room is empty. Hao An is at his stall. The
door opens and in comes Li Li. She lies down on the
bed and falls immediately asleep. She is clearly
exhausted. We have the impression that she often
comes here to sleep. Perhaps this is the only place
she can truly rest. When she wakes, she collects her
things, leaves the room and disappears down the
alley.

Late that night, when Hao An returns home, he
catches a faint scent of her in the sheets. On the
floor by the bed he finds a gold earring with a single pearl dangling at its end. This could only belong
to a beautiful creature from heaven. He holds it up
to the light. His scruffy room — his home that isn't
quite a home — feels completely transformed.

Scene 18

We've reached the critical moment in Hao An's story.
He's serving customers at his stall when Li Li
appears. She asks him for money. How can he refuse?
She is a beautiful creature from heaven! He tells her
she can have the money if she stays and helps him
out. She stays, but does very little work. However,
Hao An is happy just to know that she's there. He
gives one of his rare smiles.

That night, as Hao An leans over in bed to switch

off the light, Li Li arrives in his room. Silently, she takes off her clothes and lies down next to him. The warmth he feels is entirely new to Hao An. He wonders if this is Love. He repeats the word to him-self, 'Love', and again his body floods with warmth from head to toe.

As Li Li sleeps, Hao An stares at her silky smooth back. He reaches out and places his finger on a pur-ple bruise. He strokes it, gently, back and forth.

Scene 19

Li Li doesn't return to Hao An's stall. By day, he stares intently into the mass of people before him. By night, he stares intently at the lone earring in his hand. He tries to calculate how many hours are left before the end of the world.

Scene 20

Li Li rushes into Hao An's room and throws a stash of banknotes, rings and necklaces on to the bed.

'Hao An, you're a good man. I know you are. Help me look after this.'

Then she is gone, back out into the night.

Scene 21

Hao An's hotpot stall is being smashed up by the police because it isn't registered. Hao An walks home through the rain, dejected and wet. His abandoned

hotpot smokes by the side of the road, gradually
filling up with rain.

Scene 22

Hao An squats on the floor of his not-quite-home
looking at the earring in his hand, gold with a single pearl dangling at the end. There is a knock at
the door. A policeman. Does he know a woman called Li
Li? If so, could he come with them to identify a
corpse that has been found in a drain?

At the morgue, Hao An immediately spots the blue
tie-dyed shirt. The policeman tells him her real
name was Zhang Guilan. She was from He Bei province, Lai Yuen county, Fragrant Chives Mountain,
Knotted Peach Tree Village.

Scene 23

Hao An studies a calendar. There are still a few days
left before the end of the world. He puts some things
in his holdall and takes a look around his bare room.
Then he locks the door behind him and walks to the
long-distance bus station.

Closing scene

With his holdall slung over his back, Hao An walks
over barren hills, through thin forests of scraggly
trees, across a bleak and desolate snow-capped
land. As he nears Knotted Peach Tree Village on

Fragrant Chives Mountain he can hear sheep bleat-
ing and sees a scattering of low huts in the distance. 'Maybe I've found it,' he thinks, 'maybe this
is her home.' Zhang Guilan, the Li Li of his heart.

END

Fenfang tries to understand
the battle between
the Old Man and the Sea

ONCE YOU'VE SEEN A SHARK, you always take care when you walk into the sea. I was terrified Xiaolin would come round to my flat again, and that next time it might be my leg he broke, not just the light. Ever since the day I told him I was thinking of moving out, Xiaolin had been involved in a systematic process of destruction. First it was my work. He tore up scripts of films I was meant to appear in, and burnt my address book of contacts. Next were my tools. The contents of my pencil tin were repeatedly obliterated. Pencils. Rulers. Erasers crumbled. He crushed even the smallest things. I would come home to find mangled paper clips and staples strewn around the floor.

Not much escaped the shredding. Especially my photos. I loved taking pictures of Beijing. The rusty iron railings by the gates of the Forbidden City on a summer afternoon. A People's Liberation Army soldier, hunched over and shovelling snow in the winter. Beijing Canal clogged with so much rubbish it made me sad. Mao's portrait in Tiananmen Square framed by a sea of red fluttering flags. Old people playing ping pong, with their dogs fighting nearby… Each of these pictures was ripped to pieces by Xiaolin. I became a peasant again – living in a big city without any record of the past.

The teacher at my Modern American Literature evening class used to go on about Hemingway's *The Old Man and the Sea*. He said it was one of the most important books in the history of Western literature, and we should all read it. He would hold the book above his head and talk about the battle between the Sea and the Old Man, and how it symbolised that a man can be 'destroyed but not defeated'. Somehow, whenever I thought about Xiaolin, I thought about that book. In the battle between us, Xiaolin simply refused to be defeated.

I remember a conversation Ben and I had during the one trip we made out of Beijing. We'd only been together a few weeks when Ben told me he wanted to visit this city he was studying for his PhD. Did I want to come?

It was the first time I'd been in a plane. Thin wispy clouds drifted past the window. As I watched them, I wondered whether there really was only one universe, or if in fact there were multiverses. Would life have different dimensions in another universe? Perhaps being young wouldn't mean much there, or being in love… Ben put his arm round my shoulder and pulled me back to this universe. I realised I was truly away from Beijing. Xiaolin couldn't reach me here, not unless he'd learnt to fly. I was free of the constant sense of danger. The fear that he was going to leap out at me from behind some corner.

Ben must have been thinking the same because after a while he said, 'I wish that crazy boyfriend of yours would leave us alone.'

I was quiet. Then I said, 'Maybe you can help me, Ben.'

He took his arm away. 'Oh, Fenfang. You know I want to. But I don't know how much I could offer after a while.'

What did that mean?

'Maybe we should just run away,' I said, with hope. 'Why not? China is big. We could hide ourselves in any corner, we don't have to be in Beijing. Yes?'

Ben didn't say anything.

We travelled to Changchun, a city in the north-east, in old Manchuria. When we finally unbuckled our seat-belts and got off the plane, we entered a world of ice. It was a city of heavy industry, and it seemed like it hadn't changed since 1949, the year when China became communist. The snow was black on the ground from the muck pumping out of the chimneys.

I reminded myself that this place had played such an important role in history. The Japanese had forced the last Emperor to create a fake state here in the 1930s. He'd lived in this city, surrounded by his concubines. Ben insisted we visit the Last Emperor's Palace. It was now a desolate museum. When we walked in, there was only one other visitor, a foreigner burdened by a huge backpack, squinting at obscure old photos. It's only foreigners who know about China's history, I thought. I know nothing. But still, in that half-hour in the rotten old palace, I learnt about Pu Yi. About how he'd been crowned Emperor at the age of three. How he'd married a girl the eunuchs selected for him when he was 16. How he'd been forced to flee from the Forbidden City in Beijing. How, during the Japanese occupation of Manchuria, he tried to avoid marrying a Japanese woman imposed by the occupier. How he'd been imprisoned by Stalin in Russia. How, in 1962, Chairman Mao arranged for him to marry again, to a member of the communist party. Pu Yi. A man who had lived as a prisoner, as a citizen, as the last Emperor, and yet someone without any choice. The old man Pu Yi had obviously not defeated the sea.

Ben and I walked down a street lined with shabby shops. We ate pickled cabbage and duck-blood soup served in bowls as deep as basins. People were very generous here. It felt like any city in China was better than Beijing. We watched local teenagers skating on the frozen river, each swathed in thick padded cotton jackets. We wandered along the city's perfectly straight roads. Xiaolin couldn't reach us here. If we were to die here, in this frozen icy north, he would never know.

But the shark constantly swam back to the old man. My mobile started to ring. For some reason, I felt unable to switch the phone off. I couldn't reject Xiaolin's call.

As a compromise, I turned the sound off and felt the little mobile vibrate silently. I could imagine Xiaolin, alone at home in Beijing, slamming the phone down so hard the walls shook.

That night in the Banners and Flags Guesthouse, I woke in panic. My phone had lit up. Ben could hear it vibrating against the table edge. He opened his eyes, and we both stared at it as it twinkled menacingly in the dark.

'Just leave it, Fenfang. He'll get fed up.'

'You don't know him,' I said.

Ben looked at me. 'Why can't you switch it off? I don't understand you.'

He turned his body away, exhausted.

People always say it's harder to heal a wounded heart than a wounded body. Bullshit. It's exactly the opposite – a wounded body takes much longer to heal. A wounded heart is nothing but ashes of memories. But the body is everything. The body is blood and veins and cells and nerves. A wounded body is when, after leaving a man you've lived with for three years, you curl up on your side of the bed as if there's still somebody beside you. That is a wounded body: a body that feels connected to someone who is no longer there.

Fenfang moves to Haidian

WHERE WAS I? I sat up in bed, trying to see stuff in the dark. There was a door to the left. A bathroom to the right. Shelves over here. Drawers there. A half-dead bamboo plant on the table, and a TV by the window. The window was directly in front of me. Okay. I knew where I was now. As soon as I found where the window was, I was all right.

I was in Haidian, in my new flat. Rent: 850 yuan per month. Hassle: 0. All the other tenants in the block were either university students or professors. They were quiet and reasonable people. Everybody wore glasses and carried at least two books in their bags every morning when they left for work. There were no old hens in the elevator pressing buttons and watching your night life. Most importantly, there was no Xiaolin. He didn't know where I'd gone.

Haidian stirred me. Haidian was the greatest area in Beijing. It made my heart beat faster.

What I loved about Haidian was you could find whatever you were looking for. Banned books like *Soul*

Mountain by Gao Xingjian, or that memoir by Chairman Mao's private doctor where he spills all the dirt. A little old man sold Taiwanese Fried Ice and it was the best in Beijing. His stall had clear plastic walls. Through them, you could see bowls piled with sweet yellow Hami melon, red Western, juicy green and bright purple grapes. Crystals of brown sugar glinted. You could fill a plastic bowl with any fruit you wanted for only 1 yuan. He'd spoon snow-white fried ice on top of your fruit mountain. He'd add sticky sugar syrup on your ice. Oh, Heavenly Bastard in the Sky, nothing tasted like that.

Past the ice stall were cramped side streets where the walls were like the scales of a fish — tall shelves tightly packed with pirated disks. You could find anything you wanted here. CDs, with a hole punched into the middle by customs. VCDs and DVDs of old classics like *The Goddess* with Ruan Lingyu, Zhao Dan's *Crossroads*, even the 1940s film *Spring in a Small Town*. And so many foreign films. *Mamma Roma. Central Station. The Lost Weekend*. Plus films by Takeshi Kitano and Shunji Iwai. All piled on top of each other like firecrackers at Chinese New Year. I loved piracy. It was our university and our only path to the foreign world.

It was in Haidian that you could track down the film Ben loved most: *Betty Blue — 37°2 le matin*. It was now my favourite film too. The main character — a handyman called Zorg — inspired me to keep writing. If a lonely builder in a nothing town could eventually become a writer, then maybe an extra could one day become a Third-Rate, Second-Rate or even First-Rate script-writer. In the film, Betty is mad – a crazy woman who always wears a red dress. I thought I was like Betty, except I never wore red. At the end of the story Betty dies. I would cry every time I watched this film. Even after 15 times. I could never forget the end. Betty was dead and her man Zorg was writing alone at a table. Suddenly, his cat jumped on the table and stared at Zorg. And then it spoke. Oh, Heavenly Bastard in the Sky. The cat started to speak and it was Betty's warm voice asking Zorg, are you writing now? Zorg looked at the cat. And that was it. The End. Heavenly Bastard in the Sky! Even just think-ing about this made me want to cry.

Anyway, that afternoon I went to the Book City mall to stock up on novels by my new favourite author, Marguerite Duras. I came out of the shop with my green Eastpak rucksack bulging. *Destroy, She Said, The Sea-Wall, The Sailor from Gibraltar* and a book about her life. Heavenly Bastard in the Sky, I knew I would love Duras the moment I read the first line of *The Lover*. 'One day, I was already old, in the entrance of a public place, a man came up to me. He introduced himself and said: "I've known you for years. Everyone says you were beautiful when you were young, but I want to tell you I think you're more beautiful now than then. Rather than your face as a young woman, I prefer your face as it is now.

Ravaged."' Genius! I could feel my heart swell beneath my Eastpak just thinking about it.

I walked past street food vendors, past Beijing University students wearing thick glasses and the same Eastpak rucksacks, and past a formation of local community People's Policemen ignoring the pirate CD shop beside them. Everything was illegal, so no one could be bothered to do something legal, even the policemen. Anyway, my feet slowed at the window of an electronics store, but I didn't go in. My destination was the McDonald's opposite Book City.

McDonald's, you couldn't call it food they sold there, but they had three things you won't find in other restaurants in Beijing: 1) clean floors; 2) toilets with paper; 3) frosty air-conditioning. If you ever find yourself trying to swallow the steaming hot dumpling of a Beijing summer, make for the Book City McDonald's. It's the only place that will cool you down. When I lived in Haidian, all the locals would save money on their electricity bills by going to McDonald's to enjoy its complimentary cold air.

At the counter I ordered a red-bean ice-cream, then picked a table in the corner. Next to me was a giggling collective of teenagers, deep in conversation about TV star Little Swallow over their Big Macs. I took a lick of the beany cream, opened my Eastpak and lovingly selected one of the Duras novels.

As I was opening the book, a young man walked

towards me. Long black hair to his shoulders, bony, tall. He was like Takuya Kimura – the man from the TV soap *Tokyo Love Story*. The kind of man your eyes would automatically home in on in a Beijing crowd. He walked past me and sat at the next-door table. I had a perfect view of his broad back.

I noticed he was carrying a green Eastpak, like mine. He unzipped it and pulled out a book, as casually as if he was in his home. He breathed deeply, exhaling the pollution and tiredness of the city into bright, cold McDonald's.

Heavenly Bastard in the Sky, it was then that I saw the book he'd placed in front of him. Marguerite Duras, the same Marguerite I had in my hand: *The Sea-Wall*. I took a sharp intake of breath. The Big Mac teenagers had moved on from Little Swallow to *King Kong* and *Shrek*. I couldn't take my eyes off the man with the book. His long, pale fingers turned one page after another. Each motion he made was like someone in love, each action elegant, calm, tender. I stared at his back without blinking.

My mobile jumped. Ben's number flashed up, then a fuzzy long-distance echo passed from Boston (Latitude 42° North, Longitude 71° West, −4 hours GMT) through time and space until it landed at table number 8 by the third window on the north side of the Book City McDonald's (Latitude 40° North, Longitude 116° East, +8 hours GMT).

'Hi, Fenfang. How are you?'

'Fine. I'm eating red-bean ice-cream in McDonald's. It's so hot outside it's like Firehill in Xinjiang.'

'What? Fenfang, I can't hear you very well.'

'Hello? Can you hear me now?'

'Sorry, Fenfang, what did you say?'

'I said I'm eating red-bean ice-cream.'

'Fenfang, can you speak a bit louder? It sounds like you're in a busy playground with lots of babies screaming.'

'Can you hear me now? Okay. Good. I'm not in a playground, I'm in McDonald's. Listen, what do you think of this? "One day, I was already old, in the entrance of a public place, a man came up to me. He introduced himself and said: 'I've known you for years. Everyone says you were beautiful when you were young, but I want to tell you I think you're more beautiful now than then. Rather than your face as a young woman, I prefer your face as it is now. Ravaged.'" Isn't she a genius?'

It was so silent on the other end of the phone that I imagined Ben was listening carefully. Then he said, 'Sorry, Fenfang, I don't understand. Can you explain?'

'Forget it, Ben. The connection is too bad, let's just hang up.'

I was pissed off. When I looked up, the man with the long black hair had gone. He'd taken away his Duras. My Marguerite. He'd disappeared into Haidian with its huge population of young people and its rush of honking cars and bicycles.

FRAGMENT FOURTEEN

Fenfang tries to write a script,
            but not in Beijing, in Xi'an

I THOUGHT MAYBE I could write better if I got away from Beijing for a bit, so I travelled to Xi'an, an ancient city that was the capital of many dynasties. I stayed in the suburbs, to the east of the city, in a state-run hotel called the 'Just Like Home' guest house. Instead of signing myself in as a bit-part extra on 20 yuan a day plus a 5-yuan lunchbox, I said I was a 'Professional script-writer', and went around the hotel in dark glasses and a long black coat like Keanu Reeves in *The Matrix*, carrying my laptop.

The air in the Just Like Home guest house was stale. A dark-red carpet ran along every corridor in the building. In the daytime, the hotel was deadly quiet. There was never anyone around. Eight hundred years could have passed and still no one would have knocked on the door asking for a room. But it was different at night. At first it was as though the entire hotel slept the sleep of the dead. I would switch off my laptop, and crawl into bed with the lamp on. The mattress was unpredictable. Some nights it would stay hard; others it would cave in and I would find myself in a crevasse. Then, as I lay trying to sleep, I would hear the sound of a woman weeping. The sound would stop and then start again. It reminded me of the wailing saxophone music they used to play in Lush Life, a jazz bar in Haidian that was a favourite hang-out for foreigners. Lush Life got knocked down one or two years ago.

So there I was at the Just Like Home guest house, only a few miles away from the grave of the Terracotta Warriors. I was trying to write my script, but the noise of the night started to get to me. I began to think the hotel was a trap, a place from which people never escaped, a place where all the guests turned into dusty warrior statues. Maybe it was old Emperor Qin Shi Huang playing tricks. I was worried that I would wake up in the morning to find that I had become a dusty clay warrior too.

It might have been said that by escaping alone like this, I was not participating in the Community. That I, Fenfang, wasn't contributing to the Greater Socialist Good. But I didn't care. I wanted to hide away and write. I wanted to meet characters who would climb up my pen. I wanted to create a completely new world, inventing everyone and everything. Yet whenever I closed the door of Room 402, opened my laptop and sat in the faded red chair, nothing would happen. My thoughts would dry up. My ideas would be impossible to pin down. Room 402 would turn into a cage, rattled by the fitful bird inside.

Every morning I would wake up and pull back the stained brown curtains. Outside was a sea of state buildings from the 1980s covered in heavy yellow dust. Okay, so Beijing had dust. But this was dust that had been lying around for 5,000 years. Everything in Xi'an was covered in dust. The houses, the people. It covered each needle of the pine trees and every petal of the red canna flowers. I could almost hear the pine trees and the flowers coughing. The first thing I'd do in the morning, I'd get into the shower. I'd try to wash away the noise of the weeping woman and the vision of dust, but it echoed in my head all day. I'd get dressed and put on my long black coat. I liked my oversized coat. It covered my body entirely, protecting me from the annoying yellow dust.

In the lobby three female employees with nothing to do would be sitting at the front desk. Behind their heads were three big clocks showing the time in London, Tokyo and New York. I couldn't see why they needed international clocks since only peasants would stay at the Just Like Home guest house. Not that it was very homely. You had to be brave walking across a lobby like that, with the eyes of three women fixed on you. Especially in dark glasses and an oversized coat. I knew what would be going through their square brains. They would be thinking I was a prostitute. Why else would a young woman rent a room alone? It's not standard in China. And, in China, anyone who does something 'not standard' is immediately suspicious.

Anyway, at the door, I'd be met by the doorman, a skinny young boy all in red like a ceremonial imperial guard. Instead of opening the door, though, he would be practising martial-arts moves in front of the mirrors. Monkey Finger. Flying Limb. Double Leg Kick. Classic moves picked up from popular martial-arts films. When he wasn't busy with his routines, his nose would be pressed to the window. He'd be staring intently outside, even though there was never anything to stare at.

I'd push open the lobby doors myself and walk out into the world of dust. About 100 metres on, in the middle of all this dust, was a shabby canteen called Little Chilli Pepper. Inside was a permanent swarm of flies and three or four middle-aged men with cigarettes glued to their lips playing mah-jong. Outside was the constant rumble of lorries and tractors carrying coal from deserted west China to crowded east China. I would look down at my feet to see my shoes covered in Xi'an dust. Usually I would give up at this point, turn around and walk back to my room. That was generally the full extent of my inspirational morning walk.

I had wanted to be in a place where I could walk around and meet interesting people. Good old people. Smiling kids. Pregnant women. Gas-canister delivery men on their bicycles. School students running home in the rain. Couples arguing. Policemen dozing in their cars. Boy racers screeching past on scooters… These were the people I wanted to draw into my stories. I had wanted to find a place where I could be myself – the real Fenfang, not just some bit-part extra.

On my last night in Xi'an I had a sudden urge to see the city centre and its famous Ming-dynasty bell tower. Before I went back to brand-new Beijing, I thought it would be good to see some 600-year-old bell. So I got up from my laptop and went down to the lobby to find a taxi. It was 11.30 at night. The taxi driver sped through the streets like a maniac and then left me. I stood alone in the middle of the road. Beside me, the bell tower loomed, solemn and silent. It was so dark I couldn't see a thing. Everything around me was shut and it was impossible to find out what the bell's story was. This made me sad. Whenever I wanted to learn more about the places I belonged to, I found myself at a dead end. I sniffed. Despite the darkness, I could sense Xi'an's thick dust blowing in on the wind from over the old city wall. I spotted a light bulb ahead. I started to walk towards it. A barbecued fish stall. I sat on a wooden bench next to a few men with the same build as the Terracotta Warriors. Ancient bone structure must have run through the generations of Xi'an citizens.

I started eating splintered skewers of barbecued fish, one after another. I would finish one and lay the chewed wooden stick on the table before taking another one. My face was a statue too as I listened to the descendants of the Terracotta Warriors joking and laughing, drinking beer and eating barbecue. I finished 10 skewers. The sticks on the table were like dead soldiers in a Qing grave. I looked up. Unfamiliar streets extended into darkness beyond the stall. I held onto the table tightly, feeling as though I might drift off into the night if I didn't.

The ring of my mobile jolted me back to reality. Across the screen was a string of numbers with four zeros at the beginning. Ben.

'Fenfang, I've been trying to reach you at home for days. Where have you been?'

'I'm in Xi'an.'

'Xi'an?'

'Xi'an, you know. The ancient city of warriors made from cooked earth. I'm just having barbecue fish.'

'What? Cooked warriors and barbecued fish?'

I listened to Ben's slow voice on the other side of the Pacific. It sounded as if he were on tiptoes in front of a large map of China trying to locate me.

'Yes, I'm in Xi'an, Ben, and everything's fine. Do you want to hear the wind?'

I lifted my phone to the night sky, high up to the wind and the dust.

Soothed by the familiarity of Ben's voice, I stood up from the fish-stall bench and called a taxi. The driver was the same maniac as before and he soon deposited me outside the Just Like Home.

Back in Room 402 I climbed into the unpredictable bed and lay there listening to the sound of the woman weeping. It was like a tide coming ever closer. Suddenly I felt terribly alone. I longed to be back in Beijing. The city that had become my home. The city where I had fallen in love for the first time. The city where rice and noodles awaited me in a kitchen cupboard. I thought about Xiaolin. Beijing was where Xiaolin and I had bought orange curtains together. A 1.8 x 2-metre red bedspread for a double bed. Where we'd held hands in the cinemas in Xiaoxitan. Where we'd eaten barbecued squid from street stalls. The city where we'd argued on street corners and eventually tried to forget each other.

I thought about the days when Xiaolin and I had lived together. His tiny apartment with the two old brown cats and the white dog that was always shitting beside our bed. And I thought about his immortal old grandmother and the bottle of Eight Dragons Soy Sauce that sat on the kitchen table, 24 hours a day, four seasons a year. Thinking of that flat made me feel like crying.

I recalled what Huizi said to me: 'Fenfang, never look back to the past, never regret, even if there is emptiness ahead.' But I couldn't help it. Sometimes I would rather look back if it meant that I could feel something in my heart, even something sad. Sadness was better than emptiness.

New Year and Fenfang eats a bowl of her mother's longevity noodles

FRAGMENT FIFTEEN

THE IDEA HAD BEEN GROWING quietly inside me for some time, the idea of returning. Back to the place I had run from at 17. I'd heard the village had been transformed — like so many other quiet corners of China. Hillsides had been flattened, supermarkets had been built, roads had been laid through the sweet-potato fields. The forgotten village of my childhood had become a bustling town. Even the name had changed. It wasn't Ginger Hill Village any more, it had been renamed Great Ginger Township. My father had retired from his travelling salesman job, and my mother didn't work in the fields any more, but was running a shop instead.

It was a bitter winter day and Beijing was being battered by a violent dust storm when I wrote to my parents:

Father, Mother,

I'm coming to visit. I think New Year's Day is on February 5th. So I will probably arrive on the 4th.

Your daughter Fenfang

I wrote my telephone number at the bottom and posted the letter.

Five days later I got a call from my father – the father who was absent from my childhood. His voice was hoarse and croaky, as though he hadn't spoken since I last saw him.

'Fenfang, this is your father. We'll have the New Year's Eve meal ready for you when you arrive.'

After that call, I went straight to the train station to buy my ticket.

The train journey took three days and three nights. Oh, Heavenly Bastard in the Sky, I had forgotten how long that journey was. I thought about the first time I made it, and how it had seemed as if it would never end. I had said to myself at the time, I'll only return when I'm rich or famous. But look at where I'd got to now: as poor and anonymous as all the other nobodies in bastard China.

I watched the countless cities and small towns passing outside my train window, Lang Fang, Cang Zhou, Ji Nan, Xu Zhou, Wu Xi, Hang Zhou... I smelled the dry Hua Bei Plains, saw the muddy Yellow River, and my favourite Yangzi River. In my memory, the Yangzi was light green, but this time it was grey. Construction sites full of concrete blocks lined its banks, one after another. It seemed to me that all the rivers had become much smaller and narrower. Perhaps the next time I returned home, they would have dried up altogether like the Gobi Desert.

Throughout the journey, I could see fireworks in the

sky and hear the constant bang of firecrackers. I suddenly realised how long I'd spent in Beijing – cold, serious, restricted Beijing. I had forgotten how joyous New Year celebrations were. Was I really going home? I felt as if I were travelling through a dream.

As I was dragging my suitcase off the train, I saw an old woman with a decayed body and awful clothes. It was my mother.

I felt a knot in my throat. Before I could put my suitcase down, the tears started to come.

Mother watched me. She was surprised. She had never seen me cry before. She had no idea what was going on in my heart, and in my Beijing life. She had no idea why I suddenly wanted to visit them. Neither could she have known that I'd once moved six times in one year, that on one of these occasions I'd had all my belongings thrown out on the street for not paying my rent on time.

Mother, Mother, you know none of this.

My parents and I sat together at the round table, having our New Year meal. The TV was on in the background and the official national Spring Festival evening show was being broadcast on the state-run channel. I realised my parents had a new, 'Future'-brand TV set. It seemed much too modern and high-tech for their house. My mother explained that they'd bought it right after they'd got my letter. She said I'd need a large TV during my stay. Oh, that TV made my heart heavy.

It felt like a scene from a film, a typical Chinese family

scene. I could almost feel the Director hovering in the background, overseeing the set-up. Father, mother, daughter, sitting together on New Year's Eve, eating and watching a famous actress singing communist songs on their newly bought TV. I couldn't care less about the show. I watched my father instead. He no longer looked like a travelling salesman. He looked old. It had never occurred to me that my father would get old. But here he was, shrinking, like all the other dried-up old people in the village. He had become even smaller than me. It clutched at my heart. I lowered my head and just kept eating the food my mother put in front of me. I lifted piece after piece into my mouth. I stared down at the bowl and worried that tears might fall into it.

My parents said nothing. They were as silent as they always had been. Only the food kept coming: endless clams. People here believed eating clams brought good fortune. If women ate them, they became fertile. On the table there was every type of clam you could fish from the East China Sea: Razor Clams, Turtle Clams, Hairy Clams. Heavenly Bastard in the Sky, I would become so fertile I could give birth to 10 children, and I didn't even know if I wanted *one*.

My mother broke the silence.

'Fenfang, have some more Turtle Clams. They're good for your blood. Do you still sometimes faint when you stand up?'

I looked up at her, my mouth full of fresh clam meat.

'Don't worry, Mother, that's over. In Beijing, I eat loads of strong meat. Lamb, beef, even donkey. And I eat loads of garlic too. I'm much stronger than I was before.'

'Oh?' She looked at me. 'If you're so strong, why is your face so yellow?'

I couldn't answer. Why was my face so yellow? Because I breathed in too much of Beijing's polluted air? Because I couldn't sleep at night? Or just because I had bad Chi in my stomach? What should I say?

Mother, you know nothing of me.

That New Year's Eve, I felt as though time was flowing backwards. Fragments of the past returned too easily and it felt as if I'd never left. Despite the boom that had hit the place, everything still felt as it always had been. The same old vinegar, just in a new bottle. I stood outside the house and heard an old man cough twice as he rounded the corner. The same cough I'd heard all those years ago, same pitch, same frequency, same tempo. After coughing twice, sure enough he spat. Same rhythm, same move- ment, same speed. Even the pitiful, insect-ravaged camel- lia plant was still in its pot by the door. In all those years, how could my father still not have found some way to cure that ill plant?

The only thing that had changed was the river behind our house. It had turned into a pathetic trickle. The riverbed was covered in plastic bags and all sorts of other rubbish. Sewage spewed down from steel pipes hanging over the mud – waste from some factory.

The stars shone down on me inquisitively as if we'd met before, and I knew we had. The damp night breeze was the same that had blown across my pillow as a child. I started to worry. Those old things gained shape too easily, too quickly. I worried that this place would pull me back, that it would not let me go again. I worried that my will to survive might shrink and age here. I suddenly missed the cruel Beijing life. I missed my insecurity. I missed my unknown and dangerous future. Heavenly Bastard in the Sky, I missed the sharp edges of my life.

It wasn't until the early hours of the morning that the battle of the firecrackers died down. My parents' bedroom was silent. In the dark I fumbled for my mobile and phonecard, and dialled Boston. Shit! The goddamn answering machine. I felt a wave of fear, as though I'd been abandoned. I put the telephone down and went back to my room. I threw myself on the bed. I wanted to write Ben an email. That Nirvana song came into my head: 'Where did you sleep last night?' But there was no email here and no way for me to hear his voice other than listen to his tedious message on the answering machine. Out of my window, I could see the first, faint light of the New Year in the sky. Ben, where did you sleep last night? Where?

I lay in bed and celebrated the New Year, in silence and alone. Another 5,000 years of history were on their way.

When I woke, the firecrackers had started up again. I walked into the kitchen where my mother handed me my first meal of the New Year – a bowl of Longevity Noodles served in a ginger and pork broth. They were hot and delicious. Suddenly I remembered the song the kids here used to sing. It went like this:

Longevity Noodles, Longevity Noodles, can you teach me the secrets of life?
Longevity Noodles, Longevity Noodles, why are you always so long?
Longevity Noodles, Longevity Noodles, should I stand on the table to swallow the length of you?

I was quiet and concentrated as I swallowed the noodles. Were they long enough, I wondered, to stretch the 1,800 miles back to Beijing?

When I had finished the last of the Longevity Noodles, my mother was content, like any mother when her children eat the food she has prepared, particularly when it is the first meal of the New Year. She scooped another bowlful of noodles out of the pot, decorated them with dried lilies, and placed it in front of me. Now I started to feel desperate. These noodles were truly never-ending.

After my second bowl, my mother asked me her first question of the New Year.

'Fenfang, you said you'd been in loads of movies and TV shows, but how come we've never seen you?'

How to explain the meagreness of the roles I'd had?

How to explain the silence that was mine on screen? A shoulder here, a profile there, a face lost in a crowd.

'Well, I guess because most of those movies and shows are only on cable channels. Yes, that's it — cable. I don't think you're hooked up for it here.'

My mother looked at me. 'Really? Well, we'll have to see what we can do about that. Your father and I will have to buy this cable thing. That way we can finally see you.'

FRAGMENT SIXTEEN

Fenfang scribbles
on a napkin and wonders
whether Patton wants to get something to eat

I BOUGHT A NEW DVD PLAYER. It was a brand called 'Soni', but not 'Sony'. It seemed like a good-quality machine because it could play all the pirated DVDs I had. For instance, while I was eating my lunch, I could watch Martin Scorsese's *Casino*. Two gangsters – Robert De Niro and Joe Pesci – screaming and fighting on the tiny screen. Sometimes I wished I was a gangster, living madly, then dying abruptly one day – shot through the heart, without any preparation. That's how I wished to die.

Anyway, as I was watching, I was dipping chive dumplings and raw garlic into a little plate of rice vinegar. I was crazy about chives the same way Popeye's crazy about spinach. I couldn't survive if there were no chives in my food. Those grassy leaves had such a strong, special taste. Every time I ate them, I would imagine having my own little garden to grow chives in. In spring I'd gaze at their lovely pink flowers and, in summer, I'd make my chive dishes. As I was lost in thoughts about chives, the action on screen suddenly became very violent. I felt nauseous. I switched off the TV and decided to go for a walk. I swallowed my last two dumplings, and walked out.

In the street, I could barely keep my eyes open it seemed so bright. Maybe I'd been sleeping too much during the day lately, and my eyes couldn't take more than my 40-watt desk lamp. I felt like a prisoner just released after 20 years in a dark cell. After walking for half an hour, I realised that, apart from McDonald's, there were so few places in this city where you could sit down. For miles and miles there were only government buildings or Nokia factories or dirty restaurants with stinking toilets or without a toilet. This city was impossible. What did you do if you didn't want to go to McDonald's?

I decided to go to the Beijing Diplomat University where you could get free-refill lemon water in the café. One hour later, I was on my third glass. The place was full of college kids weighed down with jumbo Chinese–Korean dictionaries, Chinese–German dictionaries, Chinese–English dictionaries. You could really feel that, in the future, these kids were going to be running the world.

Reaching for my pen, I started scribbling on a napkin. Then I stopped. Napkins made me think of my friend Patton, Ben's old flatmate. Patton scribbled on napkins too. I wondered if his film scripts were any good. He made out that endless Hollywood producers were interested in turning his scripts into films, but, since everything he wrote was in English and I wasn't able to read it easily, I had no way of judging.

Patton loved Beijing. 'You know, even when a city looks hard and concrete like Beijing, it's possible to love it,' he once said to me. He also said that China was better at being American than America, so he would rather live in China. Weird. How could China be more American than America? I didn't get it. Anyway, Patton wore jackets and trousers with millions of pockets, and was often being mistaken for a photographer. He was always reaching into these pockets, and pulling out small notebooks and stubby chewed-up pencils. Using these, he noted down anything and everything that he found interesting, especially examples of Beijing slang. He loved the idea that 'Second Breast' meant 'mistress', that 'Sweeping Yellow' meant 'prostitution is forbidden' and that 'Cow's Cunt' meant 'absolutely wonderful'. He would carefully write these terms down in his notebooks and, if he ran out of pages, scribble them on napkins instead.

I liked Patton. There weren't many people in this world who could be boring and fun at the same time, if you know what I mean. It seemed to me that Patton and I were similar: bored all the time. But he knew how to deal with his boredom better. Anyway, there was nothing sexual between Patton and me. We were like the 'killers' in Wong Kar Wai's film *Fallen Angels*. Killers can only ever be partners or enemies. Never lovers.

Wherever you went in Beijing, you were liable to run

into Patton in some café – the 6-foot man in the corner, wearing a big brown jacket with millions of pockets and tapping away on his famous old IBM laptop. And you could be sure that his laptop would be plugged into the only available socket on the wall, the cable trailing across the floor like a vine, climbing over chic Beijingers drinking their overpriced cappuccinos, intent only on reaching its ultimate destination: Patton's messy but clever brain.

I went back to scribbling on my napkin. Maybe I should call Patton and see if he wanted to get something to eat. But he probably wouldn't want to. Patton didn't eat much, or not as much as I did anyway. You see, that was the problem: not very many people ate as much food as I did. Whenever anyone had a meal with me, they ended up spending far more time and money on it than they wanted. I knew I ate too much, but I couldn't help it. I was ravenous all the time.

In the end, I decided to give Patton a call anyway. Needless to say, he was in some café.

'Which one?' I asked, getting ready to go.

'The café in the Foreign Business University,' he said. 'The Get Ahead Café, have you been yet? They just opened it.'

'Get Ahead Café?'

'Yes. It's great here, they serve you free tea.'

'Sounds good. But don't you want to eat something?'

I could hear him hesitating.

'Well, I'm not in an eating mood,' said Patton. 'But if

you're really desperate, we can go to a restaurant and you can eat.'

'That would be great. Do you fancy Western food or Chinese food?'

'You decide, since you're the one who's going to be eating.'

I could sense Patton was getting a bit impatient with me.

'In that case, let's go to Chong Qin Gold Mountain Ma La Hotpot Restaurant on the Third North Ring Road,' I said. Heavenly Bastard in the Sky, had I been missing their spicy duck soup.

'Chong Qin Red Mountain Ma La Hotpot Restaurant on the Third North Ring Road,' Patton tried to repeat.

'No, not *Red* Mountain, *Gold* Mountain. Chong Qin Gold Mountain Ma La Hotpot Restaurant on the Third North Ring Road,' I corrected him.

Sometimes Patton's Chinese got muddled, especially with names.

'Okay, whatever goddamn mountain it is, I'll see you there in one hour.'

I was just about to leave when I realised I would have to walk past this geeky young couple perched near my table. The two of them were all over each other, spectacles knocking together, lips glued together like sticky dates. It was embarrassing to look. I tried so hard to avoid staring that I got a crick in my neck.

Spectacle Boy: What blood type are you?

Spectacle Girl: Type B.

Spectacle Boy: That's a selfish blood type.

Spectacle Girl: But you said I was nice and sweet.

Spectacle Boy: I do think you're nice and sweet.

Spectacle Girl: But now you know my blood type. You still have time to reconsider your position.

Spectacle Boy: I don't regret anything.

Spectacle Girl: If that's what you want, we can go our separate ways when we leave this place.

Spectacle Boy: I told you, I don't regret anything.

I took a deep breath and dashed past them to the door.

'The Theory of Relativity!' announced Patton as soon as he arrived at my table at the Chong Qin Gold Mountain Ma La Hotpot Restaurant. He took off his multi-pocketed big brown jacket, and put his famous laptop on the table.

'Theory of what?' I had no idea what he was talking about.

'Einstein,' said Patton. 'The Theory of Relativity. So, last month I told my girlfriend to come back and live with me. But now, of course, I want to leave her again. I can't do my own thing any more. I have to switch off the light before midnight so she can get her sleep, and I have to wake up before nine to clean the kitchen and take a shower. When I lived alone, I didn't give a damn about dirt – my own, or the kitchen's. It's like being a married couple, it bores me to death. But it's all my fault – I was the one who asked her to come back because I was scared of being lonely.'

'But, what's this got to do with the Theory of Relativity?' I was confused.

'Don't you think that is the Theory of Relativity?'

'Sounds more like the Theory of Independence,' I said.

'Whose Theory of Independence?'

'Oh, I don't know. Maybe that American President's. Didn't he write some Theory of Independence?'

'Okay, Fenfang, let's have some beer.'

But I didn't feel like having beer, somehow beer doesn't make people happy.

'What about having some sake?' I suggested. 'Sake is light, it makes you light-hearted.'

'Shit, that's way too expensive. Let's have beer, and we'll make it the cheapest one too – Revolution Beer.'

I nodded and Patton ordered us two Revolution Beers in his formal Chinese.

'What happened to that wild ex-boyfriend of yours?' he asked as he lifted the bottle to his mouth.

I thought about Xiaolin and felt like it was a story from a previous incarnation. Since I moved to Haidian, I hadn't heard from him. He didn't know the phone number of my new flat, and I had changed my mobile. My nights were no longer interrupted by the ringing of the telephone.

Without answering, I changed the subject.

'Listen, Patton, you're American. What do you know about Tennessee Williams's writing technique?' I asked.

'You want to know about Tennessee Williams? Jesus, he's as old as a dinosaur, I must have read him when I was twelve.'

'So you mean he already died?'

'Oh, ages ago. He choked on a bottle top.'

'He did what?' I was horrified.

'Yes, a disgraceful way to die. He was a very sad man. He was an alcoholic and a homosexual, his lover died long before him, from cancer. He lived almost completely alone for his last twenty years…'

Heavenly Bastard in the Sky, I didn't want to hear depressing things about Tennessee Williams. I wanted to hear about his Streetcar of Desire, and his method for writing first drafts. And if this Williams guy's life was really as tough as Patton made out, I wanted to discover that fact for myself.

I broke off the conversation and turned my attention to the menu. Summoning the waitress, I ordered us the spicy duck soup hotpot. There would be tons of chillies and garlic in the broth. Patton and I could enjoy torturing our tongues instead of dwelling on the sad life of Tennessee Williams.

Almost immediately a large, steaming pot arrived. We began sweating like the soup in front of us, and Patton started taking off layers of clothes until I could see his chest hair through his thin, damp shirt. I did the same, and kept stripping until there was nothing reasonable left to take off. The other customers just stared at us.

With his face red and dripping wet, Patton said, 'Fenfang, I have a great idea for a script.'

'Oh? Has it got anything to do with drinking duck soup?'

Patton nodded. 'Yes, definitely. It starts like this. Two aliens arrive from another planet to study humankind. They land on Beijing's Third Ring Road, take a look around, and transform themselves into an American and a Chinese scriptwriter. They're starving, so they head for the nearest restaurant, the Chong Qin Red Mountain, and order spicy Ma La hotpot. The food is so hot that they start removing bits of their equipment, until they realise they've become the centre of attention. Suddenly they get worried that their true identities might be discovered...'

'And then?'

'I don't know, I haven't got that far yet. But anyway it's about these two aliens at the Chong Qin Red Mountain Ma La Hotpot Restaurant, trying to bring some civilisation to this earth.'

'Not Red Mountain, *Gold* Mountain,' I said. My mouth was stuffed with seaweed and duck. But even as I was swallowing it, I still felt hungry, even when the food dropped into my stomach.

'I've been watching loads of DVDs recently,' said Patton. 'Every night actually.'

'Me too. It's the most popular leisure activity in China at the moment, don't you think?'

'God knows. Anyway my favourite movie last week was *The Sixth Sense*. I loved the twist at the end, when you understand that Bruce Willis was dead all along…'

'What?' I shouted, choking on a piece of duck. 'I thought Bruce was alive! How could I have missed that? Maybe I was in the kitchen cooking dumplings, or in the toilet.'

Patton seemed upset. 'How can you watch a film like that? Chinese people are terrible movie-watchers. My girlfriend is the same. She'll chat on her mobile during the most dramatic scenes. We watched *The Blair Witch Project* together. It was unbearable. Do you know what she was doing during the closing scenes, the most intense part of the film? She was on the phone to her auntie in Three-Headed Bird Village, Hu Bei province! Then, afterwards, she had the nerve to keep asking me what happened. It drives me crazy. To be honest, I think one of the reasons I tried to split up with her was because she just doesn't know how to watch a film.'

'Patton, you Americans take watching films much too seriously. It's like going to church for you. For us, going to the cinema is just the same as going to the market to buy cabbages.'

Patton didn't answer back. It seemed like he'd given up.

After that, we didn't talk much. We just stared at the steam rising from the bubbling hotpot. Some families had flooded into the restaurant and occupied all the tables. In the back room, a woman sang karaoke in a horrid voice – Sandy Lam's 'I Love Someone Who Isn't Coming Home'. These days, most big restaurants have karaoke in order to attract customers. The Chong Qin Gold Mountain Ma La Hotpot Restaurant offered free karaoke if you ate two ducks. Anyway, everyone was screaming around us, but Patton and I were as silent as two pieces of tofu. We didn't know what else to talk about. As soon as we left the dreamworld of films, we both became boring and ordinary people again.

Perhaps we should just sing karaoke.

I looked at Patton. He was as frustrated as me. I noticed the empty bottles on the table.

'Right, Patton, time for another Revolution…'

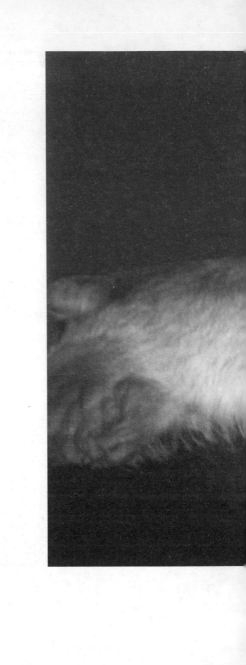

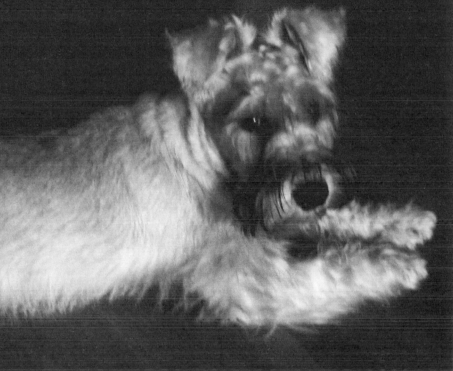

After one day in a new job,
Fenfang breaks down and calls Xiaolin

I DECIDED THAT I HAD TO GET OUT of the narrow cupboard my life had become. I found a proper job at a film and television company. It seemed time to forge my self-centred individualist life into some kind of healthy activity in an official Collective Team. The company I went to work for was called New Century Films.

The night before my first day at work, I watched the state-run TV news. I needed to know the name of the General Secretary of the Communist Party of China since I didn't read the newspapers. It was 8.30. I washed my face and decided to apply a Korean herbal face pack. I wanted to look like a fresh moonflower when I met my new Collective Team for the first time. I didn't want my face to show that I hadn't seen anyone for days, and that I'd been living in my apartment with only computer cables for company. I brushed my teeth and unearthed some dental floss that I hadn't used for about eight lifetimes. I wanted my breath to be like an orchid's when I spoke. Then it was the outfit. I turned my cupboard upside down looking for a skirt that wasn't too unconventional. I found this bullshit pink suit a costume designer once gave me because it didn't suit the leading actress. I rummaged until I found some serious-looking shoes. By 9 p.m. I had also prepared my office bag. I had no idea what an office worker should carry to an office job. I filled the bag with a notebook, a new ballpoint pen, a women's magazine. I added in all those extra women's props, a lipstick, face powder, lip pen, eyelash brush.

Getting ready like this reminded me of when I'd been a schoolgirl. Every spring, our school had gone on a trip to a mountain or a forest. The night before the trip, I would torture my poor little bag because I could never decide what to take. Then I would be too excited to sleep, and the next morning I'd be so tired I'd be late. Once I even missed the whole trip. We repeat ourselves in life – the same habits, over and over again.

By now it was 10. I needed to go to bed, to rest myself like any peasant does before starting a hard day's work in the fields. I set my alarm for 8.30 a.m. Then I decided to set the alarm on my mobile phone as well. And the clock radio. In fact, I made sure that any piece of equipment in the room that could make a noise would do so at 8.30 a.m. precisely. But then I thought: if I wake up at 8.30 a.m., and arrive at the office at 9 a.m., that might look like I don't take the job seriously enough, which would not be a good first impression to make on my new Collective Team. So I decided I should wake up at 8 a.m., and that an 8.30 a.m. entrance to the new office would be more modest. I changed all the alarms and climbed back into bed. But again, lying there, I decided no, I should get up at 8.30 a.m. because this time was more in tune with my body-clock. I needed to be honest with my body, it wouldn't be happy if it was cheated. I got up and changed all the alarms back to the original time of 8.30 a.m. By now it was 11 p.m. Shit. I lay down and tightly shut my eyes.

Snuggled up under the covers, I felt nervous and excited, like a pregnant woman. Tomorrow I'd be going to work. My first real job. I thought I should write an email to Ben, share this big news with him. I got up, plugged in my computer and waited for it to charge up. I wrote Ben a quick email, then I switched off the computer and jumped back into bed. I lay as still as I could, as though I was playing the part of a Red Army soldier dead on a battlefield, who can't move until the Director says: cut! My mind wouldn't settle. I started to think about how I should spend my first month's salary. Maybe I could buy a kitchen ventilator so I could see what I was cooking. Maybe I could also buy a vacuum cleaner to suck up all the hair on my floor, so I didn't feel as if I lived in a hair salon. Or I could just use the entire sum on phonecards to call Ben whenever I wanted. I tried to imagine where I would be sitting in the office, whether I would have my own desk. I wondered what would happen at lunch, whether I would be invited to eat with the rest of the Collective Team. And at the end of the day, how did they say goodbye to each other?

Then I started to have nightmares. In one dream I missed the subway, just like in that film with Gwyneth Paltrow – *Sliding Doors*. I was running to make it on to the train, but the doors closed just before I got there, and all I could do was watch as the train left me behind on the empty platform. The dream made me so nervous that I woke up and jumped out of bed. It was still dark. My alarm clock said 1 a.m. Far away from 8.30 a.m. I lay back down and fell asleep. That's when I dreamt of my father, or rather my father's funeral.

An undertaker was working on my father's aged face, as he lay in an open wooden coffin. Everyone was at the funeral – family members, villagers, even the Community Leader was there. But strangely, it wasn't in our village, but one by the sea. The grave was on a sharp, narrow cliff above the water. There was so little space, the mourners had to stand close together and straight like pencils. Any false move and you'd either drop into the sea or into the grave. From the cliff, you could look out over the entire East China Sea, and see Japan and Taiwan. An old man threw earth over my father's face and suddenly the eyes opened. My father looked straight at me. I felt an urge to jump into the grave to help him close his eyes, but the next shovel of dirt covered his face. I woke up. Then bang – 8.30 a.m. Every possible alarm was ringing around me. Officially summoned, I got up. Brushed my teeth.

Washed my face. Dressed carefully – knickers, tights, bullshit pink suit. I was as quick as an army cadet in training. And now, there I was, fully dressed, with my bag of props. I locked the door and walked out into the street.

I arrived at New Century Films before anyone else. I tried to make myself busy. I made tea in a big pot. I washed the teacups. I found a pile of newspapers and distributed them to each desk. Eventually, the Collective Team arrived and I was given my daily tasks. They involved taking a file and moving it into a different folder, and then taking another file and moving that one into a different folder. After that, I took a sheaf of papers and divided them up into individual files, which I then put into different filing cabinets… The whole day was spent like this. My mind wandered. I was sneaking reads of the daily newspapers on the desks. I made frequent trips to the toilet. I couldn't sit still at my desk. As soon as I heard the boss's footsteps, I would automatically bury my head in my files, but somehow my eyes just wouldn't stay lowered.

After a nervous, busy and empty day like this, I realised I couldn't stand it any longer. I quit. I made my apologies to the Collective Team and left the New Century Films office.

As soon as I slipped out the door, relief flooded over me. Now I could take off this ridiculous pink suit, wash away the make-up and not have to think about clocks the next morning. And I'd be able to sleep without nightmares, and without any more dreams about my father's funeral.

When I was outside, I called Xiaolin. I don't know why I did it, but by the time I realised my mistake, it was too late. He picked up the phone straight away. I could tell he was surprised, but he tried to sound like he didn't care. When I heard his voice, a chill went through me, but I found myself asking if he wanted to meet for supper. We agreed on a restaurant where we used to eat all the time – Lin's Fish Head near the Beijing Film Studios.

I was already sitting at a table when Xiaolin arrived. We ordered a carp's head in broth. Carp reminded me of the first time we met, when Xiaolin gave me that 8-yuan lunchbox with carp fish. Life is circular, it just goes round and round. Anyway I looked at Xiaolin. He seemed to have put on some weight. I suddenly had a vivid image of him as a middle-aged man. I started to talk. I told him everything about my first and last day in my new office job. He listened quietly. It seemed as if he was trying to prove to me that he could be different. I watched him as I talked and I started to worry. I started to panic that I would go back to him. That our life together would begin again. I felt desperate. What a crazy thing to do! What on earth had possessed me to revisit my past?

The flame underneath the hotpot licked the sticky bottom and the fish head disintegrated into a gooey mess. The fish bones had melted too. There was nothing solid left to be eaten except for the fish eyes. Xiaolin and

I talked. We talked about nothing important: the nearby construction work, the newly built Beijing TV tower, the subway plan released by the government. We were like two managers in a town planning office. It was strange. We avoided talking about relationships. And I didn't want to know anything about his grandmother, his sisters and his parents. I looked at him across the table and wondered if we could be like any other divorced couple, civilised and adult, meeting every two months to discuss their children's future.

At last Xiaolin said, 'Do you know that our white dog died a month ago?'

This was a bit of a shock. When I lived with Xiaolin, I never thought the animals in that flat would die. They seemed immortal, just like his grandmother.

'How did he die?' I asked.

'He was just too old. One day we didn't see him. We thought he had gone outside. Two days later, my grandmother found his body underneath her bed.'

I didn't know what to say.

Xiaolin paid the bill. Then we said nothing more. He drank the last drop of beer, stood up and said goodbye.

He left the restaurant, self-controlled, without turning around.

I sat alone for a while. I gazed at the fish bones melting in the pot. It had been a strange day. Xiaolin felt like the only person in the world I was intimate with. We were like family – family members always hurt each other.

And Ben was not my family, Ben lived for himself. A Western body. When Ben and I slept together, he could forget all about the love that was lying next to him in the dark. I felt he didn't need much warmth from anybody. His own 37.2° C were sufficient for him. His spirit slept alone.

I thought about how, after Ben and I made love, he'd turn his body away from me. His naked back would face me. Even though our bodies were just two or three centimetres apart, I couldn't bear that distance. I felt abandoned and sometimes, in the dark, I couldn't help myself, I missed Xiaolin. I missed nights with Xiaolin.

Huizi takes Fenfang to meet a Producer,
Comrade Loaded-With-Gold

I'D BEEN TRYING TO WRITE SINCE 10 A.M., and now it was half-past two.

'You only need to finish the first draft.' Huizi's words had been echoing in my ears. I wanted to create something exciting, but I felt whatever I wrote was lousy and trivial. Somehow it all referred back to roles I'd played in various pathetic films: Executioner's Assistant, House Cleaner, Steamed-Bun Seller, Woman on Bridge Pushing a Bicycle. I wanted to write a female character who could be everything: wife and mistress, servant and warrior, all at once. But I realised I had no idea how to do this. I didn't understand women. In all my time in Beijing, I'd never managed to have a female friend. It seemed every woman in this city was either busy with her kids or with her mortgage. Money was the only friend she needed. And I wasn't my own friend either. So I gave up on women and started writing about something else.

Very quickly I wrote a two-page outline for a film called *The Internet Artist*, copying the style from *The*

Matrix. It was about a computer geek obsessed with controlling the internet. This geek created a particularly vicious internet virus and then got himself a job as a virus-hacker. And suddenly this guy had the world at his mercy. He could do anything with the internet he wanted. He had absolute power, he was so powerful that he began to feel disillusioned and couldn't deal with what he'd done. So he tried many different ways of committing suicide. Eventually he succeeded and disappeared for ever. The world sank into chaos and horror, their master was gone...

I finished the story and called Huizi.

The story sounds all right, Huizi said. I've heard about this Producer who's got loads of cash and is desperate for scripts. I've already sent him one of mine. If I give him a call, we might be able to meet him today.

I couldn't believe my luck.

I hung up the phone and decided to make myself a hot cup of coffee. Hot coffee is like a 37.2°C man. They both give you the courage to face a new day.

An hour later Huizi and I arrived at the Producer's office. It was on the 21st floor of the Jian Wai SOHO building, where all the foreign businesses have their offices. Looking for the lift, we got lost in the massive Starbucks on the ground floor. When I saw the Producer, my heart sank with disappointment, and when I saw what was written on the business card he handed me, it sank even lower.

Jin Gui Quan, Manager of the Anti-Piracy Group.

His surname – 'Jin' – literally meant gold. Let's just refer to him as Comrade Loaded-With-Gold.

Comrade Loaded-With-Gold was a man who had worked in the fields for 30 years before suddenly making it rich. He looked like a long sweet potato, his face swollen from a lifetime of struggle, his teeth sticking out from eating endless watermelon. His skin was greasy and his forehead was heavy over his eyes. He looked newly rich and greedy. Comrade Loaded-With-Gold had a thick north-eastern accent, and never once looked straight at me, probably because I wasn't a man.

He sat back in his chair and flipped through my script. He seemed to be thinking. Suddenly he picked up his mobile phone and madly pressed some buttons. At once he started shouting into the phone about stocks and shares, about what was up and what was down. Then he hung up as swiftly as he had started, tossed his phone on top of my script and sat back in his chair. He looked in my general direction and started to speak.

'So, you're a woman writer. I, eh, I've never read anything by a… you know… woman before. And eh, don't be angry, but let me tell you women can't write. You tell me which great writer in China was a woman? There just aren't any. Qiong Yao, that writer from Taiwan, maybe she counts, if you say that Taiwan belongs to us. That story she wrote, about a little princess or a little swallow or something, that was just about okay… What I love to read are the tabloids. That's where you find some real stories, true stories. True stories are what make great writing. My favourite newspaper is *The Police Review*. And I just threw some money into making a TV series called *I Kidnapped a Woman*. Your story about the internet, why not make it from the point of view of the policeman looking for this hacker instead?'

Comrade Loaded-With-Gold took a breather, slurped some of his tea. I looked over at Huizi, but he was staring out of the window.

Comrade Loaded-With-Gold spat a couple of tea leaves back into his cup. He leant back into his chair, getting himself comfortable.

'Huiziiiiiiii, Fenfanghhhhh,' he drawled, 'let me tell you, life is really interesting. I've had so much to, eh... chew over in my lifetime. You know what? Only yesterday, I advertised for new staff and eight girls showed up – all of them over one metre sixty, all wearing the same suit, same make-up. I lined them up to have a good look at them. It was like choosing myself a concubine, heh-heh! I quizzed each one a bit, but aiya! To tell you the truth there just wasn't one that was right. What a shame! So I got rid of them all, and went out to buy a half-kilo of steamed buns instead, and aiya, wouldn't you know, as I'm standing there buying my buns, here comes this sweet young little thing and stands next to me. Aiya, this girl, I tell you, she was something! I started chatting to her.

'At first she didn't give a shit, but eh, my thick skin is my best quality, you know? So in the end I managed to persuade her to come to my office and to take the job. And you know, in my life, I've always had luck with tall women. And this girl is one metre seventy. I can't remember her name, but I remember where she's from: Wen Zhou, the smartest town in Zhejiang province.

'Then yesterday night, you know what? I'm at home watching *Palace of Desire* on TV, and she calls me! She says, "Brother Jin, want to come over to my place?" Aiya, when I heard this, I tell you my blood started getting hot, you know what I mean, Huizi? Because I've struggled, let me tell you, I've had a shit life! But I'm definitely not stupid. I reminded myself to be careful with that kind of woman. Maybe it was a trap, maybe she had a whole bunch of men at her place, waiting to kidnap me and steal my money! So I called a taxi and we drove over to the address she'd given me, and when we got there, I gave my taxi driver an extra 50 yuan and told him to take a look at what was going on upstairs. And he came back and said everything looked pretty normal, and she looked a nice girl. So I go up there myself and, well, we spend the night together. A night of destiny, I tell you! The next morning, I hand the girl 2,000 yuan, and tell her, "Go ahead, treat yourself to some nice clothes, eh?" But this girl surprises me again! You know what she says? She says, "Brother Jin, I don't want your money. Why don't we start a business together instead."

Aiya! I hear this and I'm impressed. This girl's got prospects. She doesn't want my 2,000 yuan. She's so smart, she reckons she can make 20,000 yuan instead! I put the money back in my pocket and I stop thinking that she might be a prostitute. What a brain! You know she is from Zhejiang province – that explains everything. People have sharp brains over there, and every cell in their body belongs to a business shark, not like us north-easterners with our slow pig brains… Aiya, what is she called, that girl? Really I can't remember.'

Comrade Loaded-With-Gold's mobile beeped again. He put down his teacup and answered. I didn't know which godforsaken corner of the north-east the call came from, but it went on and on and on. The extent of the conversation was Comrade Loaded-With-Gold's attempts to explain to the idiot at the other end how to make long-distance calls, but pay only local rates. I swear he explained it a hundred times, but the moron still couldn't get it.

Through all of this, Huizi and I sat still and bored to death on his sofa. It was like a punishment. I hated sitting and waiting, but I didn't want to walk around, either. The ridiculous office had four red-leather sofas with four plastic bamboo trees standing in each corner. I guessed *four* must be Comrade Loaded-With-Gold's lucky number.

Outside the window I could see the sky darkening already. A sand storm was coming. The strong smell of leather was making me nauseous. Huizi kept looking back and forth between me and Comrade Loaded-With-Gold. My outline lay neglected on the table.

Finally Comrade Loaded-With-Gold hung up and turned his attention back to the pair of us. Without much of a pause he resumed his life stories.

'You know, life is really something. I've been told that by the time I die, I'll have been in love four times. This girl from Zhejiang province, she must be one of the four. I could give you some ideas for scripts, Fenfang! Let me tell you about my first love. You're not going to forget this, eh. At middle school, I was in love with our class prefect. She was a giant, this girl, so tall! Aiya, it gave me goosebumps just to look at her. When our term finished I wrote her a note saying, "Hey, why don't you sit next to me in the back row next term?" I know I'm short and she was very tall, but I tell you, even then, I knew I had luck with tall girls. We were all out skating on a frozen lake, and I slipped this note into one of her red gloves, which she'd dropped on the ice. And then I stuck around, I didn't want to miss her reaction! And you know what happened next? She was coming back for her glove when she fell, and slammed right into the ice! Oh, I tell you I felt terrible! Finally she pulled herself up and used her red gloves to dust herself off, and there, out from the glove, flew my note! She picked it up and read it. I was watching intently, but no reaction. She just put the note in her pocket. And then you know what she said to me as she walked past? She said, "Gold, you have dirty, dirty thoughts. We're too young to think like that!" This was a harsh criticism, and from my very own adored giant of a class prefect!'

Comrade Loaded-With-Gold's mobile beeped loudly once again. He looked at the phone and got suddenly quite agitated.

'Aiya, I think it's that girl from Zhejiang. And I remember her name now too: Zhang something. But let's forget about Little Zhang... Let's talk about us now.'

It surprised me that he was ignoring the call. 'We should get some food, eh. There's a place downstairs called Friendly North East. They make the best pork intestines, just delicious...

'Yeah, so where was I? Oh, after the class prefect criticised me, we never spoke again. Forty years passed and then one day, I'm on a visit to my old home town, Ha Er Bin. I'm driving my BMW along a street when I spot this stall selling fresh pigs' trotters. "Those will be perfect with a bottle of beer for dinner," I think and, aiya, you'll never guess, even in your next life, who I see behind the stall! My old class prefect! But, I tell you, eh, what an awful sight she was. Fat, like a Buddha! With an annoying little kid beside her chopping pickles. She must have been twice as wide as me! But her name... her name, I remember it now: Li Yaqin. Li Yaqin grabbed my hands and started fawning all over me. "Aiya, Gold, it's you! How do you come to be here? All these years

I've been searching for you! I have had such a difficult life. My father's been working in the mines and I've never had any money. Aiya, I so regret what happened, Gold."

"'What do you regret, Li Yaqin, eh?" I asked, and she started to cry, just like that! Clutching at me and telling me that the happiest moment in her life was the day she fell on the ice and read the note I'd written her. "I was so happy!" she said. "And all these years I couldn't find you, but now here you are, with your big car at my food stall! But it's just too late, and my boy he's so big now." At that moment, I looked down at the pigs' trotters and you know what? They looked just like her hands – dark and fat and stained.

'Aiya, life… you know. Life is just like those stewed pigs' trotters. Sometimes you just have to eat what you're given.'

At this point Comrade Loaded-With-Gold's eyes started to mist over. Huizi and I looked at each other, and neither of us knew what to say. My outline was still on the table, completely abandoned by now.

Comrade Loaded-With-Gold suddenly raised his head from his sentimental past and looked at me.

'Fenfang,' he drawled. 'Tell me, do you find a man like me interesting?'

Huizi shot me a look.

'Sure, really interesting.' I cleared my throat. 'Yes, definitely. I find it really easy to relate to you, especially since you're about the same age as my father. It's not that difficult to understand you.'

I could feel Huizi relax.

'Aiya, you meet me for the first time and already you think I'm fascinating, eh. Well, that Wen Zhou girl, aiya, what's her name… you know?'

'Zhang?' I offered.

'Yes, yes, Miss Zhang. Right, well, I can't chat any more, you see, I should go and ring back Little Zhang.'

And with that, Comrade Loaded-With-Gold walked out of the red-leather office to make his call.

Huizi and I both stood up, perfectly synchronised. I picked up my outline from the desk and shoved it into my backpack. I didn't blame Huizi. We walked out of the office.

Another sand storm was starting, the wind flapped at my thin skirt. There was never any gentleness in a Beijing spring. Huizi and I walked and walked. There was silence between us. A woman passed us on her bicycle, she'd wrapped her scarf over her mouth to stop the sand. Men carrying their evening newspapers and briefcases hastily pushed past us. Comrade Loaded-With-Gold's north-eastern accent still rang in my ears, as did those words… 'Dirty, dirty thoughts!' Sand whirled up into my eyes and I couldn't stop rubbing them. My head ached.

Huizi could sense I was a bit low.

'Right, Fenfang,' he said, 'I'm taking you to Jade Pond Park to see the cherry blossom.'

I just said, 'Okay.' Nothing more. Then I followed Huizi. I can't explain why, but I felt like I'd aged five years since walking into Comrade Gold's office. I actually felt lots of sympathy for the man. As I'd said to him: I understood him.

Jade Pond Park, with its famous cherry trees, was packed with tourists. You could hardly move. Parents with their children. Young people with their old parents. Visitors, officials, builders, guards. We climbed up a little hill to get a better view. The trees spread below us were like sculptures made of twisted wire, the pink blossoms were swinging in the sand-filled wind. There was hardly any scent.

I thought of Japan and how popular the cherry-blossom season is there. Then I remembered a sad story I read in the newspaper about a young Japanese girl who had committed suicide by jumping into a waterfall. In the note she left, she explained:

I don't want to lose the beauty of my youth. I don't want to see my body ageing. The cherry blossom chooses to die in one night. I want to do the same.

I looked again at the cherry-blossom trees beneath me and saw that the grass was already covered by a layer of fading petals.

Fenfang receives a phone call from
an Underground Director

'LIFE IS JUST LIKE those stewed pigs' trotters. Sometimes you just have to eat what you're given.'

Comrade Loaded-With-Gold's words stayed in my mind. He was probably right.

As for stewed pigs' trotters, I didn't even have those. I hadn't worked for two months. There were no frozen dumplings in the freezer, no rolls of toilet paper in my bathroom, no soy sauce or vinegar in my kitchen, no soap by the bath. I'd used everything up. Worse than that was the loneliness of it. I put the kettle on to boil. I could feel a headache starting again. This always happened when I hadn't had any coffee for a few days. I rummaged around and found a sachet of stale instant. My worst worry was what I'd find in the sugar bowl. I closed my eyes and opened the Taiko sugar tin. Heavenly Bastard in the Sky, sure enough, there wasn't even any sugar in this place. Instead there at the empty bottom were two dead cockroaches, starved to death.

I sat at the table. For half an hour, I just sat and slowly drank the bitter coffee from my big cup. When I had finished, nothing had changed. But my headache was going away.

I started hunting through my clothes for money. I searched my pockets and even my winter coat from last year. The tiniest bit of loose change was enough – anything to get me through the day. Altogether, I managed to find 25 yuan.

I went downstairs and immediately tasted sand in my mouth. The air smelled dusty. I ran into the nearest store and bought one pack of frozen chive dumplings, two packs of instant noodles and a tin of sugar. Five yuan change. As I walked home, I prayed for rain to arrive to help this desert city. 'Please rain,' I murmured. 'Please rain, please rain, please rain.'

Back in the apartment, I wolfed down a bowl of instant noodles and drank another cup of coffee, with sugar this time. Then I sat at my table, contemplating my telephone. Something was bound to happen, someone had to come to save me, I could feel it. 'Please help me, please help me, please help me...' I whispered. Two minutes later, the phone rang.

Heavenly Bastard in the Sky, thank you! It was a call about money. A call from an Underground Director!

The Director introduced himself. It was such a long introduction that I almost fell asleep. He took me through the story of his struggle to be a cutting-edge artist from A to Z. In the beginning, he'd wanted to be mainstream, to be accepted by the state, maybe even get to Hollywood. But when he finished his first feature, for some reason it never got past the censors. So he changed his politics and decided to become an Underground Director. The more films he made, the more underground and angry he became.

Anyway, as I said, I was just about falling asleep when the Underground Director said he'd heard about this film called *The Seven Reincarnations of Hao An*. He said he thought Hao An sounded very underground and his seven reincarnations pretty intriguing. Could he read the script?

Could he read the script? Underground Director, you are my Bo Le and I am your horse. I am 1.2 million per cent happy to give the story of Hao An and his Bloody Mary Li Li to you.

The Underground Director was happy too.

'Great, great. All right, Fenfang. Come and meet me tonight. Nine o'clock. Huai Yang Cuisine on the second floor of the Jiang Su Hotel.'

More than fine! I hung up. The Heavenly Bastard in the Sky never seals off all the exits — there's always a way through. In this world there must be more than 300 different ways to die, but who cares. At least I wasn't going to die of hunger.

At 8 p.m. I set out for the Jiang Su Hotel, script in hand. I could feel a fever growing in my head. My throat was sore and my ears ached. The sand storm outside felt like it was taking me over. I could hear grains of sand hitting the windows of nearby buildings and I felt as if, at this moment, my whole future lay in my hands. I was so terrified, I needed to talk to someone to get a hold of myself. I took out my mobile and phonecard, and called Ben. Thank the Heavenly Bastard in the Sky, this time it wasn't the famous answering machine.

'Ben, Ben!'

'What is it, Fenfang. I'm just brushing my teeth and I've got to be in college in fifteen minutes.'

I could hear running water in the background. I suddenly started sneezing and coughing.

'Sounds like you've got a cold, Fenfang. Did you go to the doctor?'

'What?' I sniffled down the line. 'Don't be ridiculous. Chinese people can't go to see the doctor every time we have a stupid cold.'

'Well, if you won't go see a doctor, then at least buy some cranberry juice, it's good for fevers and colds,' said Ben impatiently.

'Cranberry juice? Are you crazy? In all of Beijing, you can only buy weird stuff like that at the Jian Guo Men Friendship Store and the supermarket under the China World Trade Centre. There's no way I'd be able to afford it. Thirty yuan for a taxi there to buy a tiny bottle of some extravagant American juice that will cost about forty yuan!'

Ben got impatient again. 'Whatever, just take care of yourself, Fenfang.'

'Okay, okay, I will. I just wanted to say hello to you. There's a crazy wind out here today. Sorry, I have to go now, I'm in a hurry.'

'Me too,' said Ben. 'Speak soon.'

I put my phone back in my pocket. I suddenly realised the whole business with Ben just didn't make any sense. Why did we carry on talking on the phone? Didn't we realise there were 18,400 miles between us? Couldn't we admit that we knew nothing about each other's lives? I didn't even know how old Ben was, or what his family was like, or whether his parents were together or divorced. As for Ben, he had no idea where Ginger Hill Village was, or of how I had dreamt of a different future. I felt desperate.

With so little money in my pocket I couldn't get a taxi. I had no choice but to get the bus halfway across Beijing, through Ditan to the Jiang Su Hotel. My shoes were dusty from all the people stepping on my feet as they squeezed on to the bus. My long hair was full of knots. I'd forgotten to put on make-up and I was wearing an ugly coat to protect my body from the spitting sand. I had none of the charms a woman should have when she goes out to meet a man. But fuck all that fake stuff, what did it matter here anyway? I was going to meet an Underground Director. A real one. A seriously anti-mainstream guy.

I had to change buses twice. I could feel my temperature rising. It was already after nine o'clock, but still the buses were so packed the conductor couldn't get through to collect the tickets, and kept shouting. My head was throbbing, and the script in my hand was getting crumpled. When I finally managed to extract myself from the jammed bus, I moved like an old dog. I could see the Jiang Su Hotel towering ahead of me. I was cold and hungry. Be patient, be patient, I kept repeating to myself. Soon you'll get Hao An's story made into a film and you'll earn enough money to buy hot duck soup every day.

I hurried up to the second floor and found the Huai Yang Cuisine restaurant. But there were no men on their own. I looked around and around. No sign of anything like an Underground Director. Had he left already? What if I wasn't going to get any money today? I bent over the bar, grabbed a phone and punched in the number he'd given me.

'Hey, it's me, Fenfang. I'm here! Huai Yang Cuisine on the second floor of the Jiang Su Hotel. Where are you, Underground Director?'

'I said the Jiang Su MOTEL, not Jiang Su Hotel!' he said. 'You need to take a bus a couple more stops.'

Who the fuck would put a Huai Yang Cuisine in the Jiang Su Motel *and* in the Jiang Su Hotel? Desperately, I hung up and ran back downstairs into the dark night.

As I hurried into the street, I felt my body temperature jump from 36.5°C to 37.2°C and then keep on going straight up to 39.5°C. I was having trouble breathing, it was like an asthma attack. Everything around me went blurred. I couldn't tell the difference between the Jiang Su Hotel behind me and the Jiang Su Motel ahead of me. The buildings looked the SAME, the characters on the signs looked the SAME too. The wind persevered in its howling and the moon had disappeared behind the sand swirling in the sky. It was the end of the world. I could still just about hear the latest news being broadcast via the loudspeaker hanging on the electricity pole:

Again, a violent storm has taken our city by surprise. According to the Beijing Meteorological Centre, at 4 p.m. today the concentration of sand in the city's air reached a peak of 1,012 milligrams per cubic metre. This evening a gale-force-eight north-westerly wind reached the Haidian area of the city. The storm originated in the Gobi Desert region of Inner Mongolia and will continue on its course into northern China, before making its way south...

The weatherman's last few sentences were drowned out by the sandy wind. This was Beijing. A city that never showed its gentle side. You'd die if you didn't fight with it, and there was no end to the fight. Beijing was a city for Sisyphus – you could push and push and push, but ultimately that stone was bound to roll back on you.

The wind was as solid as a pot falling on my head as I stumbled through the streets. A man trembling in the cold passed me, so I asked him the direction to the Jiang

Su Motel. 'What motel?' he barked at me, with clearly no idea where the hell it was. He pushed past. An idiot. 'Life is just like those stewed pigs' trotters. Sometimes you just have to eat what you're given.' Heavenly Bastard in the Sky, I was repeating Comrade Loaded-With-Gold's words again.

The neon lights of the high building in front of me gradually focused into characters, a name, a motel, the Jiang Su Motel. Heavenly Bastard in the Sky, it wasn't an illusion, I was there.

That night I sold Hao An's destiny and received 5,000 yuan from the Underground Director. As I was leaving, he said to me, 'Fenfang, I never expected you to be so young – or to have such a red face and hot hands. You look like you could play the Bloody Mary woman in your story.'

I thanked him and then I thanked him again, before I sank into the darkness of the stormy Beijing night.

FRAGMENT TWENTY

Huizi says: Fenfang, you must
take care of your life

TWELVE BOXES ALL TOGETHER, small and big, I counted.

I sat on the edge of my bed, looking around the empty room. Everything was packed, and the storage company was coming tomorrow morning. This place was half dead. A naked bulb was dangling from the ceiling. A broken plastic chair standing alone by the door. Two packets of instant noodles past their sell-by date abandoned on the table. The broom propped silently in a corner. The walls marked where I had taken down the posters. It was strange to see how memories can be packed into boxes – 10 years of living in Beijing wrapped up in cardboard. Tomorrow, all these boxes would be stacked into a warehouse. Tomorrow, I would receive a piece of paper with a number. Then I could go anywhere I wanted, travel anywhere without worrying about paying rent. That number would be my home, the digit home in my brain.

Perhaps I would go to Yun Nan in the south, and live on a mountain. I could ask the locals to teach me how to find mushrooms in the forest. Or I could go to Da Lian, the seaside town, and discover the Yellow Sea and its fishing boats. Or perhaps I could go to Mongolia, to live in a tent, look after sheep and lie in the grass looking up at the big sky. But before going anywhere, I needed to get hold of the script for a play, a play by Tennessee Williams called *A Streetcar Named Desire*. Heavenly Bastard in the Sky, I was determined to know what this Tennessee guy was all about. I wanted to see if I could find the shiny things in life all by myself. I wanted to know if I could sleep by myself and not yearn to feel next to me the warmth of a 37.2°C man. While I thought about all this, I toyed with my address book, opening it, flipping from beginning to end, and back from end to beginning.

Finally I called Huizi. He was the only person I wanted to see before I disappeared from Beijing.

'Hey, Fenfang. I was just about to call you to say goodbye! Where shall we meet?'

Silence while we both thought about this.

'Jazz Ya!' we yelled at the same time. It was the only old bar left on Sanlitun Bar Street after they demolished the whole area.

I arrived at Jazz Ya before Huizi. It was early evening, there weren't many people around. Behind the bar, a DJ was playing cheerful Japanese pop. I sat at a table and listened to the music. For the first time in ages, I felt patient. I wasn't in a hurry. When Huizi came in, he looked a little sad. Was he sad about me leaving? I didn't ask. Without saying anything, he ordered tequila. A moment later, a glass arrived on the table. Heavenly Bastard in the Sky, it was the smallest glass I'd ever seen in my life. And there wasn't much in it, either. The clear liquid barely wet the bottom.

I scanned the menu: *Gold Tequila – 30 yuan.*

'Huizi, Huizi, why not just drink ten bottles of Revolution Beer? It would cost the same!'

'No, today I feel like drinking this,' said Huizi.

I had never seen this kind of drink in Beijing before. A slice of lemon perched on the rim of the glass. Huizi went through some bizarre motions. He put some salt on the back of his hand, licked it off, then grabbed the slice of lemon, sucked it and downed the tequila in one. A glistening wet mark was left on the table. Then he banged the empty glass back down.

A waitress walked past. 'Another one!' Huizi called after her.

A moment later the girl slid back with another Gold Tequila. Another 30 yuan – I did the sums in my head. Golden consumption. He performed the whole action again, salt, lemon, empty glass. Another watermark appeared on the table.

As I watched Huizi, I couldn't help thinking of a film I'd seen by Billy Wilder – *The Lost Weekend*. It's the story of a man who desperately wants to be a writer, but ultimately he's too much of a boozer to write anything. His full-time job seems to be to drink. This drunkard writer never gets further than the title on the first page: *The Bottle… The Bottle… The Bottle…* Huizi was not like that at all. Huizi knew how to write.

By now, he had finished his sixth tequila. The glass sat back on the dark wooden table beside six watermarks.

We both sat quietly and surveyed the shining wet circles. An abstract landscape. Something was in my throat and in my mind. Ever since I'd known Huizi, I'd wanted to ask him a question. It was now or never.

'Huizi, what keeps you alive? What is it that you care for in life? No, actually, that's not what I mean.' I tried to find the right words to describe what it was that really bothered me.

'Can you tell me, how can you be so at peace, steady as a stone in a forest, while I'm just nervous and desperate all the time?'

Huizi looked at me without answering. Perhaps my question was too big, too vague.

'You know what I mean, don't you?'

'Yes, I know what you mean,' said Huizi. 'But I can't answer. I don't actually know. But sometimes a very small thing can touch me for a long time. Like that poem by Cha-Haisheng, "Facing the Ocean, the Warmth of Spring is Blossoming". It's beautiful. If I don't feel all right sometimes, I will think of the ending of that poem:

Name each river, name each mountain
Name them warmly
Stranger, take my warmest blessings
May your future road be clear and bright
May you be reunited with your true love
May you find real happiness in this dusty world
I will face the ocean, waiting for spring to warm the air
   and flowers to blossom.

'When I think of those lines, my heart is warm,' said Huizi.

I listened in silence. Then Huizi said something unexpected.

'Fenfang, I need to tell you, I used to love you, and now… I still love you.'

The rings of water on the table glistened.

I said nothing.

Huizi left Jazz Ya soon after that. It was not his style to leave so abruptly. But he said he felt drunk and he had to go. Before he left, he reached for my hand and held it hard. It was strange, I realised we'd never held hands before. His fingers were slim and long, but his palm was fleshy and warm. It was a strong feeling.

The last thing Huizi said to me was, 'Fenfang, you must take care of your life.'

The next day, I left Beijing. I bought a one-way ticket to Shan Tou. I wanted to smell the South China Sea. As I sat on the rattling train, Huizi's words echoed in my mind. They echoed through the years I had spent working as an extra, the dead years when I made tin cans and swept floors. They echoed through the streets of a forgotten village.

I am 17 and it is a sweltering summer morning. I open the creaking shutters and look out at the hills. Rows of sweet potatoes stretch into the distance. The silent fields shimmer in the heat. I contemplate the pale clouds collecting in the sky. It's time to leave. The unforgiving sun is melting my youthful body. I tell my 17-year-old self: *Fenfang, you must take care of your life.*

Acknowledgements

It feels as if I, my translators and editors have run a marathon to bring you this book. It was the first novel I published in China, and I wrote it when I was very young. Ten years later, when I began to collaborate on the English translation with Rebecca Morris and Pamela Casey, I realised there were two major obstacles to turning it into a book in English.

The first was the language. The translation needed to capture the speech of a young Chinese girl who lives a chaotic life and speaks in slangy, raw Chinese.

The second obstacle was that I was no longer completely happy with the original Chinese text. Ten years on, I found I didn't agree with the young woman who had written it. Her vision of the world had changed, along with Beijing and the whole of China. I wanted to rework each sentence of my Chinese book, and fight with its young author who knew so little about the world. Although Fenfang, the heroine of the novel, should still be desperate about her life, I wanted to convince her to become an adult.

To rewrite a Chinese book when it has already been translated is a big burden to place on a translator. The only way to do it was to write in English over the top of the translated text. Fortunately, my editor Rebecca Carter understood what I was trying to do.

So, I have been spending a lot of time with three Western women, chasing a language for the elusive Fenfang. Throughout the process, I have been caught between two cultures, fighting for a common world between two languages. Now that we have crossed the finishing line of this marathon, I want to dedicate this book to two very special people: my editor Rebecca Carter and my agent Claire Paterson, who mean so much for my writing. And to Michael Wester: I hope you can accept this novel as a long-overdue gift from me, wherever you are and whatever you think of Fenfang. An eternal thank you to Philippe Ciompi for his soul and his heart. Then I would like to thank Alison Samuel, Clara Farmer, Juliet Brooke, Rachel Cugnoni, Audrey Brooks, Suzanne Dean, and all the Chatto & Windus and Vintage team in London, as well as Lorna Owen and Tina Bennett in New York and Cindy Carter in Beijing. And finally, thank you to my two youthful translators. We are now coming of age, and I am very grateful to all of you.

Xiaolu Guo
Hackney, June 2007